AT RISK

REBECCA YORK

OLIVERHEBERBOOKS

Cover design by Dar Albert, Wicked Smart Designs

Published by Oliver-Heber Books

This title was previously published

0 9 8 7 6 5 4 3 2 1

CHAPTER ONE

Rafe Gascon felt his stomach muscles knot as he loitered in the shadows, staring across the street at the restaurant called Chez Eugenia, the last place in the world he'd expected to find himself.

From his vantage point, he watched patrons enter and disappear behind the lace-curtained front window. Others were already inside, eating dinner before the big show.

He snorted. Show!

It wasn't exactly a dinner theater performance. More like a very dangerous game that Eugenia Beaumont had no business playing. He'd like to march across the street, clear everybody out of the restaurant and sit her down for a very pointed talk. But giving advice on how she ran her business wasn't part of his job description. Using his special talents to protect her was.

He cast his gaze up and down Dunlop Street, on the lookout for the mugger who had recently assaulted a couple of her patrons. There were a few people on the block. A man in sandals and a sports shirt. A woman in a business suit carrying a briefcase. A young couple holding hands. Nobody struck him as suspicious, particularly the two old ladies who had gotten out of a car a few doors down from the restaurant. He assumed from their descriptions that the short, portly women were Gertie DeLong and her sister Martha Wilson, both on his list of frequent Chez Eugenia patrons. Both were well off but always on the lookout for bargains. Probably they didn't want to miss the tasty appetizers Eugenia served before the real fun started.

Rafe had kept a semblance of objectivity from his post across the street, but when he saw the restaurant owner step forward to greet them, his heart clunked inside his chest. He hadn't seen her in eight years. She was a big part of the reason he'd left New Orleans and had only come back for short visits with his dad before he'd passed. Now he would have to deal with Miss Beaumont again. He had pointedly avoided keeping track of her over the years since he'd left, but his briefing folder had filled in any blanks he'd wondered about. He knew she'd gotten married a few years after he'd left, to a guy named Richard Delaney—probably someone she'd met on the country-club circuit—then divorced after another few years. Too bad she still didn't have the husband. That would have made it easier to work with her. There would be no question that she was off limits.

From the shadows, he watched her look left and right, probably scanning for the mugger who had been screwing with her customers.

Rafe's throat tightened as he silently acknowledged that she was just as lovely as he remembered. Her pale blond hair was pulled back and secured at the base of her neck. And her oval face was flushed, probably from working in the kitchen before coming out to greet her patrons. She was wearing a beaded green flapper dress that she'd probably picked up at one of the retro shops that he knew she loved to patronize.

You wouldn't think she was in trouble by looking at her, but she'd contacted the New Orleans office of Decorah Security for help with the mugger problem. When Frank Decorah had offered Rafe the assignment, he had requested not to be sent there. But Frank had insisted, and here he was.

As Eugenia Beaumont turned and surveyed the dining room of her restaurant, she ordered herself to relax. But there was simply too much riding on this evening. Until the mugging incidents last month, Chez Eugenia had been on the fast track to culinary success. Her catfish bisque and her sweet herb-flavored crème brûlée trio had been the must-eat dishes of the New Orleans foodie crowd. And reviewers had praised the restaurant's decor, with its old brick walls, old-time photos and potted greenery.

Now she was the talk of the town for exactly the wrong reasons, and she was paying for ads on Facebook and in the local paper assuring everyone there was no danger in coming to Chez Eugenia.

Of course, you wouldn't know there was a problem this evening. The restaurant was filled with customers—as it usually was for her monthly Voodoo Night, featuring one of the city's up-and-coming voodoo priestesses, Calista Lacoste.

The arrangement had seemed like a good idea nine months ago. Now it was adding to Eugenia's anxiety. And to put the icing on the cake, so to speak, this evening she was doing two jobs. Jenny Princeton, who usually greeted guests, had called in sick. So Eugenia had done a lot of cooking early in the day and left her sous-chef, David, to finish up the meals. Lucky for her that he'd worked for some of the best restaurants in town and knew his way around a professional kitchen.

"So good to see you," she said to Gertie and Martha as she collected the seventy-five-dollar admission fee which she would split with Calista. The two sisters stopped to chat briefly, then bustled toward the back of the restaurant, heading for the food table set up along one of the side walls.

Eugenia watched them pick up plates from the antique sideboard she'd taken out of Mom's attic when she'd started furnishing the restaurant.

She glanced over the group of people seated casually at her polished wood-topped tables, some with bases made from old sewing machines. Two more good customers, Martin Villars and his wife, Holly, were here. They always made a point of telling her how good her food was, and she also knew they'd recommended the restaurant to friends, because some new patrons had mentioned it. But most of the people here tonight had come to dally with the dark and dangerous—in a setting they knew was safe.

Although she'd grown to respect the religion, voodoo wasn't Eugenia's particular cup of tea, and before the muggings had started, she'd thought about discontinuing the monthly feature. Now she was glad to have the business.

At several tables were visitors to the Big Easy who must have read about the ceremony in the ad Eugenia had placed in a local entertainment guide. And in the back was Jillian

Hargrave who had started coming to the Voodoo Night a few months ago. She was a blond in her late twenties, but she always dressed as if she wanted to play down her delicate good looks rather than enhance them. Tonight she was sitting alone, hardly eating anything.

When Eugenia heard someone clear his throat, her attention refocused to a middle-aged guy wearing dark slacks and an expensive knit shirt standing at the hostess station looking around like he wished he were somewhere else. He scuffed a shoe against the floor as he asked in a voice barely above a whisper, "Is . . . this the place where . . . uh . . . they're having the voodoo ceremony?"

"Yes."

The woman with him was short and redheaded, although it was clear the coloring was covering up a lot of gray. She was wearing a sundress and sandals, standard attire for tourists who weren't used to the New Orleans heat.

When Eugenia confirmed that this was indeed the place, she giggled nervously. Hopefully she wouldn't do that during the main event. She might think voodoo was a New Orleans sideshow, but the priestess who would be performing the ceremony didn't agree. If Eugenia knew anything about Calista Lacoste it was that the woman was serious about her religion.

"I want to tell my friends at home all about this. Do you have zombies?" the redhead asked.

Eugenia fought not to roll her eyes. "Are you referring to an animated corpse?" she asked politely.

The woman drew in a quick breath. "A what?"

"An undead being—like in a horror movie."

"I don't know exactly what I meant. I thought . . ." she raised one shoulder. "You know. That zombies might be part of the goings on."

"I'm sorry to disappoint you."

"No, no. I'm sure it will be fine. Can we take pictures?"

"No flash," Eugenia said, pretty sure that the pictures wouldn't come out well in the dimly lit restaurant.

"And the seventy-five-dollar cover charge is for hors d'oeuvres, wine and extra personnel," Eugenia said, gesturing toward the table at the side of the room where she'd set out a selection of finger foods, including some of her Cajun specialties. Splitting the fee with Calista meant Eugenia wasn't making a lot on the evening, but the cover charge would more than pay for the food and wine.

The woman glanced at her husband. "Is that all right?"

"Anything for you, honey."

Eugenia collected a hundred and fifty dollars in cash. Turning back to the door, she tensed as she spotted another man who had obviously been listening to the conversation.

He had entered so unobtrusively that she hadn't even noticed him; but when she saw his face, she went very still.

Even as she told herself it couldn't be him, she knew Rafe Gascon was standing in front of her, as tall, dark and even better looking than she remembered. And totally at ease, she noted, with the part of her brain that was still capable of drawing conclusions. A far cry from the teenage boy who'd been unsure of himself in the Garden District house where her mother still lived.

He took a couple of steps forward, and they stood facing each other for the first time in eight years. Momentarily disoriented, she clamped her fingers over the edge of the nearest table. Up close, his features were the same, although harder and a lot more worldly. And probably the crinkled lines at the edges of his eyes weren't from laughter.

"Rafe?" she asked, speaking a name she hadn't uttered in years.

"Yeah."

She fought the sense of disorientation that threatened to swamp her. "I thought you were in the army."

Rafe was struggling with his own problems, like the sudden inability to draw a full breath. Since arriving in town the day before, he'd been putting off the moment when he was going to have to face Eugenia Beaumont.

Swallowing to ease the sudden dryness in his throat, he answered, "I've been out of the army for a couple of years. I'm with Decorah Security. You hired us to investigate the muggings around here"

"Oh. You're a private detective?"

"Yeah."

Of course, when she'd hired Decorah, she couldn't have been thinking that her old boyfriend would show up. Did he sound like he was daring her to ask for someone else? If she said she didn't want him, he could report back to Frank Decorah—and get out of this assignment that was making his skin prickle.

Instead, she said, "That's fine," even when he suspected it wasn't true. Probably she'd be on the phone to Frank in the morning. But right now she needed the security she'd hired— and the investigative skills Rafe had acquired, courtesy of Uncle Sam.

He'd gotten into the MP's in the army and made Captain in the investigative unit before meeting Frank Decorah. The man had been very persuasive about recruiting him and had been willing to wait until Rafe's enlistment was up.

Standing a few feet away from Eugenia Beaumont, Rafe struggled to maintain the professional demeanor that had never failed him before. This woman had meant more to him than almost anyone else in his life. Too bad she hadn't gotten fat and ugly and ill-tempered since their teenage days. Instead she had matured into a lovely woman—and one with determination. She was out on her own, with none of her rich family members roping in their society friends to patronize her restaurant. And when she'd seen an unorthodox opportunity to bring in more business, she'd taken it.

He'd thought she might be better off with another Decorah agent. Now he understood that he wanted to get her out of trouble. And really, the moment Frank had sent him the computer file on her and he'd read about the mugging, his heart had started to pound. Even though he hadn't been sure how he was going to deal with her on a personal level, he'd taken the job because if someone was hurting her, he wanted to stop them cold.

Which didn't make it any easier to work with her, considering all the baggage they shared, although he realized he had gained an advantage in the relationship, at least temporarily. He'd known about the assignment for a couple of days. She was just finding out she'd be dealing with her old—what? He couldn't exactly say lover because they'd never gone all the way. But they'd done just about everything else.

She was speaking again, and he snapped his attention back to the present.

"Would you like something to eat?" she asked, falling back on the manners that were second nature to her. Her mother might be determined to make sure everybody knew the family was New Orleans gentry. Eugenia was a lot more down-to-earth. She'd never been a snob. She'd even let herself . . . get involved with the handyman's son.

He thrust that last thought from his mind and answered, "Not while I'm working. I want to keep my full attention on the crowd."

A look of alarm crossed her features. "You're not expecting any trouble in here, are you?"

"No, not specifically," he reassured her.

"Good."

She turned away, and he looked over the people at the tables, some of whom had arrived before he'd taken up his position across the street. When he spotted Martin Villars leaning over to say something to his wife, Rafe fought to keep from clenching his fists as he confronted another piece of his past—one of his all-time least favorite memories, in fact.

Villars had owned a couple of antique shops in town, as well as some other businesses. When Rafe had been in high school, he had made some extra money on one of Villars' furniture moving crews—until a garnet brooch had gone missing, and the man had accused him of taking it.

He hadn't of course. One thing his father had taught him was honesty. Not necessarily out of moral conviction but because stepping outside the law could get you in bad trouble.

The cops had been called in to scare the shit out of the kid they thought was a thief—including a strip search in Villars' office. Rafe hadn't been concealing the brooch. In fact, Villars had found the piece of jewelry in a drawer of an antique secretary. But Rafe had never gone back there to ask for work again. He switched from hauling furniture to frying chicken at Popeyes. You might burn your hand with splatters of hot grease, but you did get to bring home the biscuits that weren't sold before closing time—a nice side benefit in a home where dinner might be peanut butter and jelly sandwiches.

As Rafe stood near the door, Villars looked up to see who had come in. When recognition dawned, the older man's jaw firmed.

Rafe stayed where he was until Villars had turned around again. Then he wandered over to a table of voodoo paraphernalia, including ritual candles, some small boxes that could have been for jewelry, a life-sized plastic skull, and an ornate silver dagger with scrollwork on the handle. To give himself something else to focus on, he picked up the knife—and knew instantly that he'd made a bad mistake.

The scene around him wavered, and suddenly he was no longer in Eugenia's restaurant. Instead, he was standing in the bayou, under the shade of huge cypress trees, hearing the sounds of birds and smelling a mixture of damp vegetation and blood in his nostrils. The knife was in his hand, and he was kneeling over a dead goat lying on an altar, its throat slit and dripping.

He made a strangled sound as the scene sucked him in.

He was supposed to be finding out who was causing trouble for Eugenia, not taking a side trip to another time and place.

But he wasn't without some control. Before he went any farther into the altered reality, he made a concerted effort to open his hand. His muscles relaxed, and he managed to drop the knife back onto the table.

As soon as he broke the contact, the bayou scene flicked out of existence, and he was back in the restaurant again.

He looked up to see if anyone had noticed his momentary absence and found Eugenia staring at him. When he glanced away, she crossed to his side, a look of concern on his face.

"Did . . . that thing happen again?" she murmured.

He didn't have to ask "what." He knew they were both talking about his paranormal ability.

"Yes," he admitted. "What did I look like?"

"Like you were daydreaming."

"Sorry."

"Not your fault."

"I've got better control over it than when I was a kid," he bit out."

She was one of the few people besides Frank Decorah and the other detectives at the agency who knew about his extrasensory talent—the ability to pick up an object that belonged to someone and go into a time and place where they had been. It was never when the person was doing anything routine, like eating dinner in a nice restaurant or taking a stroll down the street. It was always something sharp and traumatic—or incriminating.

The talent came in handy in his work. In an investigation, he could usually direct the process. But it could also happen at inconvenient times. Like now. Or was the vision somehow connected to the assignment? Was there more going on here than a series of muggings outside Eugenia Beaumont's restaurant?

"Are you all right?" Eugenia asked.

"Yes."

He saw her swallow hard as she looked from him to the knife and back again. "What did you see?"

He didn't particularly want to discuss it, but he was working for her, and she had the right to the information. "Someone had just sacrificed a goat in the bayou. On a wooden altar. I guess with this knife." He gestured toward the dagger.

She shivered. "Who was it?"

"I don't know. It's always from my point of view. In this case, the person holding the knife."

Eugenia nodded and hesitated for a moment, ready to hit him with another question. But she probably saw that he didn't want to discuss the experience and went over to one of her customers.

At the moment, he was annoyed with himself for not keeping his attention focused on business. But he grounded himself pretty quickly when the kitchen door opened, and he saw a striking looking, light-skinned African American woman standing regally in a simple white gown and white headdress. She wasn't tall, but she managed to create that illusion as she commanded the attention of everyone in the room.

It was Calista Lacoste. She'd become prominent after his time, but he'd researched her in his report on Eugenia's background. In addition to conducting voodoo services, she had a business in the French Quarter—a shop called Galaxy that sold voodoo paraphernalia and charms—along with tarot cards and books on palm reading and astrology. You could go there for something mild and slip into heavy-duty voodoo.

Six assistants followed her into the dining room. The two men were practically naked in short vests and wide loincloths made of colorful African kente cloth. The four women were dressed in white shifts. The men carried what he knew were called djembe drums. Primitive looking, they were as much a work of art as musical instruments. The women had tambourines.

A hush fell over the room as the talent spread near the back wall, the men taking their seats on the wooden floor. In the absolute silence of the room, they began to drum, a primitive rhythm that filled the restaurant.

The female attendants remained on their feet, dancing and shaking their tambourines in time to the drumbeat.

One carried a large birdcage with a live chicken that squawked and clawed at the bars as though it knew it wasn't going to like the conclusion of the ceremony.

Jesus, what were they planning to do, slit its throat and drip the blood in the bowl sitting on the table beside the knife? Or was the priestess going to fudge the ending to the ceremony? At least it wasn't a goat, like he'd seen in the swamp vision.

Rafe stayed out of the way, leaning against the wall, working to keep his expression neutral. He'd gotten into a lot of tight situations in his life—everything from working security for live-cobra charmers to looking for runaway kids in crack houses—but never anything quite like this.

As Calista swayed farther into the room, obviously conscious that all eyes were on her, Rafe scanned the audience, judging their reactions. The priestess's gaze flicked to Martin Villars, and for a moment their eyes locked. Was there something between them, something personal? Or was she just checking out a potential patron?

Rafe studied the audience again, then came back to Calista as she moved to the rhythm of the drums and tambourines. The sexual element of the performance was unmistakable. Maybe the women didn't feel it, but he'd bet every man in the room was responding to her.

When she turned to face the patrons, the music and the dancing came to an abrupt stop. For a moment there was complete silence before she raised her arms above her head. A smile flickered on her lips as she saw that she had everyone's rapt attention.

"I am pleased to see so many of you here tonight."

Rafe switched his attention back to the audience—judging their reactions. Some of them seemed to be grooving on what they'd already seen. Others looked apprehensive, and some were more embarrassed than anything else. The middle-aged guy who'd been one of the last to arrive looked like he was thinking about making a run for the door. When his wife put a restraining hand on his arm and whispered to him, he settled back in his chair.

The drumbeat started again, and the dancers circled the priestess as she raised her voice. "Voodoo is an old and honorable religion born in Africa but encompassing many traditions. There is power here, if you open yourself to what may be. Do not dismiss what is strange to you. Let yourself merge your soul with the great collective consciousness."

The background rhythm became faster and more insistent, and the priestess moved toward the audience, lifting her hands again.

"Join us. On your feet! Become part of our celebration of life."

As she spoke, she reached for the hand of the guy who'd been embarrassed.

He tried to protest, but his wife urged him onto the floor, and he stumbled into the open area where he stood frozen for a moment, looking uncertain.

As the priestess whispered something in his ear, he began to sway awkwardly to the rhythm of the primitive music. The wife got up and joined him, along with some of the others.

The moves looked so out of character for the majority of the participants, that Rafe had to bite his lip to keep from grinning. Yet at the same time, he picked up on a kind of unsettling vibration in the air. It was like when he'd touched the knife. Well, not exactly. He wasn't transported anywhere, but he could imagine that they were in a clearing in the bayou, not a French Quarter restaurant. But it was more than that. He couldn't shake the feeling that something bad was going to happen.

Rafe glanced over at Eugenia, who had taken a position on the far side of the refreshment table. Probably a good move if you didn't want to get chicken blood on your clothing.

As he watched, the priestess moved to the birdcage.

Opening the door, she reached for the fowl and held it high. And strangely, it had stopped protesting.

Everybody's attention, including Rafe's, was focused on the priestess, so that a noise from the other side of the floor took a moment to register.

As Rafe's head swung away from the main event, he saw one of the men in the audience clutch his throat with one hand and claw the air with the other.

Sweat soaked his white dress shirt, and a film of perspiration beaded his forehead.

It was Martin Villars. He made a strangled sound, looking wildly around, then grabbed for a chair to steady himself. Instead he and the chair tipped over, both landing on the floor at the same time.

CHAPTER TWO

The drums and tambourines went instantly still, leaving an eerie silence in the room.

Eugenia's mouth went dry as she watched the scene around her turn from ceremony to chaos. She tried to weave her way toward Martin Villars, watching as his wife screamed and went down on her knees, hovering over him.

Rafe broke the stillness as he shoved his way toward the fallen man.

"Move back. He needs air."

From the corner of her eye, Eugenia saw that Calista had dropped the chicken she'd been holding and that the suddenly unattended bird was flapping around the room, squawking and looking to make its escape.

Weaving her way through the crowd, Eugenia crossed to Rafe who was kneeling beside Villars. The older man lay with his eyes closed. He didn't appear to be breathing, and his skin was pasty.

Calista came down beside the stricken man. "Can I help?

"Do you know CPR," Rafe asked.

"No. I was offering help from the loa."

He snorted, then spared Eugenia a quick look. "Call an ambulance."

He was already doing chest compressions as he gave the orders.

Ordering herself to steadiness, she gave Rafe a tight nod, then scrambled to her feet. Using the phone at the hostess station, she called 911.

"What is the nature of your emergency?"

"We have a restaurant guest who's lost consciousness—under unusual circumstances."

"You suspect foul play?"

"I . . . I don't know. We were having a voodoo ceremony," she blurted.

After putting down the phone, she looked across the room at Villars, praying that something had changed. But he lay unmoving as Rafe leaned over him, expertly performing chest compressions, singing "Stayin' Alive" under his breath to keep the rhythm.

When a loud squawking noise to her right distracted her, she saw that one of the drummers had cornered the chicken near the refreshment table. Calista came over and helped him get the bird back into the cage.

Everybody else—including Villars' wife—were silently watching Rafe work on the stricken man. Holly was twisting the ornate antique ring she wore. Crossing to the older woman, Eugenia laid a gentle hand on her shoulder. "Let Mr. Gascon take care of him. He's with a detective agency, and he knows what he's doing."

Holly nodded numbly and allowed herself to be led a few feet away, where she plopped into a chair, reached for a glass of water, and took a couple of quick swallows.

Eugenia turned to the rest of the patrons.

"Let's all sit down."

There were murmurs around the room as her guests complied. But Calista had drawn apart from the others, her gaze fixed in the distance as though her mind had gone somewhere else—something like when Rafe had had his out-of-body experience before the ceremony. Maybe she was willing herself away. Eugenia wished she had the luxury of doing something similar, but she had to stay in charge.

An eternity passed before she heard the sound of a siren in the distance. Finally the paramedics rushed into the room. Rafe gave them a brief description of what had happened, then got out of the way. Crossing to Eugenia, he cupped his hand around her arm.

"You did good—getting the onlookers calmed down."

His touch was light and his voice was low, but she was grateful for the contact.

"I needed to be useful," she answered, moistening her dry lips enough to speak. She didn't look directly at Rafe because she was thinking how wonderful it would feel to have his arms around her right now, even when she knew she shouldn't be letting her thoughts drift in that direction. He'd walked away from her a long time ago, and he was reassuring her now because he was just doing his job, not because there was anything personal between them.

She dragged in a steadying breath and let it out. "What about Martin. Villars?"

"I think he's not going to make it," Rafe answered.

"Did the paramedics say what happened?"

"No."

A death in her restaurant was all she needed after the damn muggings, but that thought was far too self-serving. Before she could dredge up something to say, Rafe started running across the dining room, dodging tables and knocking over a chair. She saw him leap through the door, into the kitchen. When he emerged, he had a firm hold on one of the drummers. The guy's eyes darted from side to side, as though searching for an escape route.

Like the chicken, Eugenia thought.

"Sit down," Rafe ordered.

"I ain't got nothin' to do wid this," the man muttered, looking at Eugenia like he thought she was going to come to his rescue.

"Then you've got nothing to worry about," Rafe said.

The man snorted.

"I'd like to leave," a voice called from the crowd. It was the woman who had wanted to meet a real-life zombie.

"Sorry," Rafe answered. "Everybody stays until we find out what happened."

"Who are you to give me orders," the guy he'd dragged back into the dining room protested

"I'm restaurant security and can make a citizen's arrest if I have to. Sit down."

The man gave him a threatening look, but he stayed put.

Rafe kept his eye on the would-be escapee as he stroked a hand down Eugenia's back. "Hang in there."

"I'm trying. Someone just died in my restaurant, and I can't help feeling responsible," she blurted.

His gaze narrowed. "What are you saying, exactly?"

She flapped her arm in frustration. "Only that he came here for Calista's ceremony. And it was obviously too much for him."

"It was his choice to be here. He could have had a heart attack for all we know. Or an embolism. The same thing could have happened to him at home."

"I guess so."

Rafe looked like he was going to say more, but a loud sobbing sound from nearby caught their attention. Holly was coming in the front door, her eyes wet with tears.

Eugenia quickly went to her, and Rafe was right behind.

"I'm so sorry," Eugenia began.

"It's not your fault." She looked outside. "Those men wouldn't let me go to the hospital with Martin."

Eugenia went to the hostess station and took a tissue from the box inside, which she handed to Holly.

The woman wiped her eyes. "Thank you."

Rafe stepped closer. "Is there someone who could take you?"

She turned toward Eugenia. "Can I call my friend, Sylvia?"

"Of course."

She returned to her table, retrieved her purse and pulled out her cell phone. Eugenia led her to a quiet corner to make the call and waited to make sure that the friend could come.

When she turned back, Rafe was speaking to the other guests. "I know this has been a disturbing event, and I want to thank you all for your cooperation. We may need to ask some questions later. Please write down your name, address and telephone number."

"What if we don't live in the city?" one of the tourists asked.

"Put the name of your hotel."

"But I'm supposed to leave tomorrow."

"I believe that will still be okay, but you'll have to check with the police."

Another tourist raised his voice. "You can't keep us here if we had nothing to do with what happened."

Rafe turned toward him, his own voice firm. "You can leave as soon as I get your information." He turned to Eugenia. "Do you have some paper?"

She produced a sheet from behind the podium, and he handed it to the man next to him. "Write down your name and address; then pass the sheet around the room."

When the man began to write, Eugenia breathed out a little sigh, grateful for Rafe's presence. If he hadn't been there to keep a firm hand on the situation, the restaurant probably would have emptied out, and there would be no way to contact the out-of-town guests.

She looked around to see how everyone was doing. Jillian Hargrave, who had been at a table for one, was now sitting with Gertie and Martha, probably because she didn't want to be alone in this suddenly disturbing situation.

Eugenia walked over to the three women. It looked like the events of the past few minutes had bonded them together.

"I'm so sorry this happened," she murmured.

"It's not your fault, dear," Gertie assured her.

"I wish I could offer you something to eat, but under the circumstances, I don't think I can."

"That's perfectly understandable," Martha said.

Eugenia looked at Jillian whose face had turned paper-white. "Are you all right?" she asked.

"Yes, I didn't expect . . ." Her voice trailed off.

"We've all had a shock. Can I get you some water?"

"Yes, thanks."

Eugenia went into the kitchen and brought an unopened bottle of spring water and three glasses to the table.

"Thank you so much," Jillian said as she twisted the top off the bottle and poured water into the glass, then took a gulp.

Eugenia nodded and looked around to see Rafe running his cell phone over the names and addresses of the patrons, photographing the information.

He had just put his phone away when the door opened and another man wearing an expensive pin-striped suit stepped into the room. She heard Rafe swear under his breath as the newcomer strode over to him.

Oh shit. The cherry on top of the sundae, Rafe thought. The police. And not just any cop, but Gordon Cumberland. From the way he was dressed, it looked like he'd graduated from patrol officer to the detective squad.

His gaze flicked around the room, spotted Rafe and stopped. For a moment he looked confused. Then a look of recognition bloomed on his narrow face. He had been the cop who had come to the antique shop when Villars had called to accuse Rafe of stealing the brooch.

After that, the guy had kept tabs on him. He was a hard-ass who thought all juvenile delinquents should be locked up, and it didn't help that Rafe had been involved in a couple of minor incidents that had drawn the cop's notice. Like when he and a kid from a rival school had gotten into a fight after a football game. Cumberland had been the cop who showed up —again. Rafe had the feeling that the history they had together wasn't going to make the next few hours any easier.

"I want to know exactly what happened here," Cumberland said.

Eugenia stepped forward. "I'm Eugenia Beaumont, the restaurant owner."

Cumberland gave her a long look. "As in the high-society Beaumonts?"

She took a quick breath. "If you want to put it that way; but how is that relevant? And why are you here?"

"I heard the emergency call and checked with the hospital. The man is dead."

Eugenia sucked in a quick breath. Cumberland kept his gaze on her for a few moments before turning to Rafe. "What are you doing here?"

"I work for Decorah Security. We were hired to keep an eye on Chez Eugenia."

"Why?"

"There have been a series of muggings in the area."

"That's police business."

"The police haven't found out who's doing it," Eugenia interjected.

Cumberland must have realized he was getting way off topic. Turning back to Rafe, he said, "Since you're on security detail, why don't you tell me what happened here?"

The way he said it implied that Rafe was making up the assignment, or maybe Eugenia had hired him for show to make it look like she was protecting her customers. Ignoring the tone of the man's voice, he said, "As you heard over the radio, a voodoo ceremony was being held here, and one of the participants had some kind of attack and died."

Cumberland turned to look at Calista and the men and women she'd brought with her who were all clustered at one side of the dining room. "What kind of ceremony?"

"We were asking the aid of the loa."

"The voodoo gods?"

"Yes."

"In an upscale restaurant?"

"The gods are welcome here."

Cumberland snorted, then inspected the chicken in the cage. "What's that for?"

"Part of the ceremony."

He shook his head as though he couldn't believe what he'd walked into.

"Do you still want a summary of the events?" Rafe asked.

"Yeah."

He began filling the detective in. At the conclusion of the

statement, Cumberland looked around at the assemblage. "We'll continue this down at the station house."

"The detective is ready for you."

Eugenia stood up and followed a uniformed officer down the hall at the North Rampart Street police station. When she stepped through the doorway into what looked like a grubby nine-by-nine-foot room, Cumberland gave her a long, considering look; and she had to stifle the impulse to smooth her wrinkled dress.

Instead, she kept her gaze steady as she sat down in the hard metal chair across the scarred table from him.

"Do you have a list of the dishes you served tonight?"

"It's in the restaurant kitchen."

"And the ingredients."

"I have the recipes."

"We've also taken samples of all the dishes on the buffet table."

Eugenia went very still. She'd come in here telling herself she had nothing to be afraid of, and he was starting off with major intimidation. Not so much because of what he'd said but because of the way he'd said it, the way he'd done in the restaurant when he'd been talking to Rafe.

She dragged in a breath and let it out, telling herself it was a reasonable question.

"Are you saying you think there was a problem with my food?" she asked, managing to keep her voice even.

"One of your patrons is dead."

"Was . . . was he poisoned?"

"The autopsy will tell us."

She hadn't done anything wrong, she told herself again. But as she took in the 'got ya' expression on his face, a terrible thought struck her. "Is anyone else sick?"

"Not that we know of."

She let out the breath she'd been holding. "Thank God."

Cumberland shuffled through the papers on the table in front of him, then took another line of attack. "You had an illegal alien working in your restaurant."

Her rejoinder was instantaneous. "That's impossible. I'm very careful to make sure everyone has the proper documentation."

"It was one of Ms. Lacoste's drummers."

So that's why the man had tried to run out. Only Rafe had dragged him back.

"Well, he wasn't working for *me*. We didn't discuss our personnel with each other."

He dismissed her answer and went on to yet another topic. "What were you thinking when you agreed to have a voodoo ceremony in your restaurant?"

"I was thinking it would bring in new customers."

"How did that work out for you?"

She sidestepped the question with, "Voodoo is a legitimate religion."

He laughed. "Yeah, and my mother is the Virgin Mary."

When she didn't respond, he asked, "What's your financial arrangement with Ms. Lacoste?"

"What does that have to do with anything?"

"Are you refusing to answer?

"We split the cover charge."

"So you're having a religious ceremony, but you charge admission. Isn't that more like a sideshow?"

"Revival meetings pass the hat. In this case, the money covers the cost of the food—and the . . ." She started to say "entertainment" but switched to "attendants."

"How long have you been holding these ceremonies at your restaurant?"

"Nine months."

"It looks like they brought you bad luck."

She had had the same thought herself. Moreover, she knew he was baiting her.

While she was mulling that over, he asked, "Did you make an attempt to keep people away from the victim?"

"Of course. Except for Rafe . . . Mr. Gascon. He's trained in CPR."

"The two of you have a history, don't you?"

"We knew each other when we were younger. We haven't been in touch in years."

"Strange that he showed up tonight."

"What's that supposed to mean?"

"I guess we'll find out."

"Are you trying to say we cooked up some plot?"

"Did you?"

Eugenia answered with an emphatic "Of course not."

Cumberland kept his gaze on her for a long moment before shuffling his papers together. "You can go, but don't leave the city."

CHAPTER THREE

As a PI, Rafe had known a lot of good cops—and others like Cumberland, who liked to make it clear that their position gave them power over ordinary people. Too bad he'd been listening to the 911 calls. After hauling everyone to the station house, he'd probably he had gone through a mental process of deciding who would be the most uncomfortable sitting around in the police station waiting to be interviewed. Since he'd figured Rafe would stand up to the waiting the best, he'd taken him first. It was a short interview, focused on the same questions he'd answered earlier at the restaurant—plus some probing into his past.

"You had some problems with Villars when you were a teenager."

"As you discovered, I did nothing wrong."

"You left town not long after that."

"Not long? It was more than three years. I waited until I graduated from high school and joined the army."

"Why did you leave?"

"I didn't see a future for myself here."

"Yeah, I thought you'd end up on probation. Like your old man."

Rafe tensed, then ordered himself not to react. He heard himself saying, "He had a streak of bad luck. He straightened himself out."

Cumberland made a tsking noise. "Robbing a hardware store is bad luck?"

Rafe pressed his lips together. He wasn't going to explain that at the time his father hadn't worked in a couple of weeks, there was nothing to eat at home, and the contents of the cash drawer had simply been too tempting.

When he didn't take the bait, the detective asked, "So why are you back now?"

"I was trained as an investigator by the army. Decorah Security recruited me a couple of years ago, and they assigned me to this case."

"This case?"

"The muggings."

"You're saying the New Orleans PD can't handle it?"

Rafe knew the question was the equivalent of 'have you stopped beating your wife.' Anything he said was going to be wrong.

He shrugged. "I do my job."

Cumberland had continued to try to get him to make a wrong move. He'd hung tight and finally made it back to the waiting area.

He asked if Eugenia had been interviewed yet, and when he found out she was still cooling her heels waiting for Cumberland, he'd retrieved his Sig from the front desk and taken a cab back to her restaurant where he picked up his rental car. Now he sat in it across from the entrance to the station, waiting for her to come out.

He saw Calista leave, walking with her head bent. Probably Cumberland had given her a nasty grilling.

And probably the civilians had all gotten off easy. Although, if someone had really poisoned Villars, and he hadn't died of natural causes, anyone could have done it.

Hanging around gave Rafe plenty of time to think. Cumberland had brought up his run-in with Villars—and his leaving the city. He'd said he saw no future for himself, which was certainly true. What was he going to do, work his way up to Popeyes manager? He'd done well in the army. When he'd gotten out, he could have joined a local police force anywhere he'd wanted to live.

Instead, he'd bumped into Frank Decorah at a law enforcement conference. Decorah had struck up a conversation after a session on investigators using their intuition. He'd liked the guy, and when Frank had offered him a job when his tour was up, he'd decided it was good idea.

Intuition? Had Frank suspected Rafe had something beyond what most detectives could rely on?

His mind went back to the first time he'd left his own body.

He'd been thirteen and starting to mature, and probably the hormones triggered a change in his brain.

He'd been walking down an alley when he saw something interesting put out with a load of trash—a bike with a slightly bent front fender. Someone was throwing it out, and maybe he could take it home and fix it. When he closed his fingers around the handlebars, the scene around him vanished. He was somewhere else. On a road out in the country, pedaling along, unaware that a car was coming around the curve too fast, heading straight for him. But he found out pretty quickly, when the vehicle loomed in front of him. Whoever had been riding the bike swerved off into the weeds at the side of the road and landed with a splash in a drainage ditch. And Rafe had slammed back into his own consciousness, shaking, disoriented, and terrified. That first time and a few times afterwards, he hadn't understood what had happened, and there was no one he could talk to about it. Certainly not his father whose brain was tied firmly to the reality around him. It would have taken longer for Rafe to figure out what had happened if he hadn't read a science-fiction story about a guy with the ability to touch things and get impressions of the people that had held them. That was similar to his newfound power—except that he got more than impressions. He went back in time—to a memorable event in someone else's life.

Sometimes he could go for months without an incident. And sometimes it was an invaluable tool in solving a crime. At first he'd had no control over the experience once he got there. Then he'd found that his own consciousness could be a secondary participant. He was someone else, but Rafe Gascon was still there.

He got up and stretched his legs, wondering what Cumberland was hitting Eugenia with. While he was waiting for her, he pulled out his cell phone and dialed Pete Grady. Rafe and Pete had grown up together in Bywater. The two of them had gotten into some scrapes together, and they'd been friends up until Rafe had left town.

They hadn't kept in touch because Rafe had cut his ties with the city when he'd left except for his father. But he was pretty sure Pete would talk to him.

He kept an eye on the door, watching for Eugenia to come out. Then he dialed his old friend.

Pete was still on duty and picked up after three rings.

"Detective Grady."

"Hey. This is Rafe Gascon."

"Rafe. I could ask what you're doing here, but I already know."

"Yeah."

"It sounds like you got into something with your old friend, Cumberland."

"Unfortunately." He dragged in a breath and let it out. "I'm with a company called Decorah Security. We specialize in unusual cases."

"Like a society restaurant owner getting mixed up with voodoo?"

"Yeah, like that," he answered, although that wasn't precisely the reason he'd been hired. He cleared his throat. "We probably shouldn't talk about it over the phone."

"Right."

"We could meet for coffee tomorrow morning, and you could fill me in on what you've been doing since I left town," Rafe said, although he had a folder on Pete's career in the NOPD. And his friend undoubtedly knew Rafe's main interest was in tapping into a source of information about the Villars case.

"How about Café LaBret around seven?"

Rafe remembered the place. Its beignets were as good as Café du Monde and breakfast that was better than the Magnolia Grill. But it wasn't as pricey.

"Sounds good."

He hung up, glad he'd made the contact. Although he wasn't going to jeopardize the man's job by pressing too hard, he wanted a source of information in the police department—in case Cumberland decided to do something stupid—like setting up Rafe Gascon and Eugenia Beaumont for a murder charge.

He glanced at his watch. It was after eleven. Too bad Eugenia was getting the third degree in there.

As he waited for her, he couldn't stop himself from thinking about the past—his and hers. They'd met when he'd gone to her house with his father to help out with a brick patio the old man was building in the Beaumont backyard. There had been a lot of bricks to carry and a lot of sand to haul, and Rafe had been the one doing most of the heavy lifting.

The project had taken three days, and Eugenia had come out to watch—and to bring them lemonade and some things she'd baked. Pecan pie. Blueberry muffins. Even back then, she'd been a good cook.

They'd started talking, and they'd been attracted.

He wasn't the kind of boy she usually met, and she certainly wasn't the kind of girl who went to his downscale public school, but they'd gotten to talking. Her polished blond good looks had drawn him. And maybe she saw him as a dark and dangerous bad boy who could spice up her sedate society life.

At any rate, she'd asked him if he could help her set up a "clubhouse" in the loft of the detached garage at the back of her parents' property. He'd agreed, and they'd ended up spending a lot of time there together—in activities none of their parents would have approved of.

He'd wondered if she'd back away if he tried to kiss her, but he'd taken the chance, and she'd responded to him.

He had a lot of vivid memories of those days. Although he'd never gone all the way with her, they'd done just about everything else.

Since coming back to town, he'd tried not to think about their close encounters. Now as he waited for her to emerge from the police station, he remembered the feel of her soft lips against his. The honey taste of her and all the steps they'd taken toward intimacy.

He'd been a horny kid back then, but he'd been respectful of her, partly because she was Miss Beaumont and he was the handyman's son. But as she'd accepted the things they were doing, he'd gotten bolder. He remembered the first time he'd unhooked her bra, then reached to the front of her, cupping his hands under her breasts, feeling their wonderful softness in his palms and the tightness of her nipples. He'd stroked his fingers across those wonderfully firm tips, feeling himself get so hard he could barely breathe.

He remembered the first time he'd slipped his hand past the elastic waistband of her shorts and into her panties, touching the most intimate part of her body. She'd been hot and moist, and the feel of her had thrilled him. He remembered when she'd finally dared to close her hand around his cock and squeeze him.

Both of them had been pushed to the limit by then, and he remembered the first time they'd made each other come—each of them—hesitantly at first—telling the other what was going to work for them.

He was hard now as memories of those teenage intimacies assaulted him. He knew he had to think about something else. But he couldn't stop himself, not yet. He'd lain on top of her, naked. His cock pressed to her silky underpants because putting it inside her was the one thing she wouldn't do with him—which was probably a smart decision because getting her pregnant would have been a disaster. They'd come that way and just about every other damn way you could do it. He knew the taste of her clit. He knew what it was like to thrust a finger into her as he brought her to climax with his mouth. And he knew what it was like to almost reach climax in *her* mouth, because she'd always finished him with her hand.

He hadn't protested because he wasn't going to press his luck. Which was considerable, as far as he was concerned. He'd taken everything she would give him and given her all the pleasure he could with his hands and mouth. In the process he'd learned a hell of a lot about pleasing a lover.

But all good things had to come to an end. As spring of their senior year approached, he knew he had to make plans for the future.

Dad had taught him most of the handyman skills by then. Rafe could replace the flushing mechanism in a toilet tank, spackle damaged drywall, get the leaves out of gutters, build and put up shelving, even take down or build interior walls. He could make money that way, and the work was satisfying because you saw the results of your labor immediately, but he'd seen his father scramble to get jobs and seen him work at cut rates and have trouble making the rent or putting food on the table when none of his regular customers needed anything done.

He'd decided he had to find a more secure profession for himself—a real career and not a series of projects that depended on the whims of others

With no prospect of going to college, he'd seen ads on TV that made sense to him. Join the army and learn a marketable skill. Most guys might have wanted to fly helicopters or shoot big guns. He'd been thinking that he'd be a good detective. Maybe his special talent would even help him. And the weapons training he'd get wouldn't hurt.

He knew the army had an investigative service, and he'd aimed at getting into that.

When he'd told Eugenia his plans, he'd seen sadness in her eyes. Although it had killed him to leave her, he'd known he had to do it.

He got rid of his arousal by thinking about how she'd hurt him—and why. He didn't actually know why. He supposed that after he'd left, her high and mighty society queen of a mother had persuaded her not to keep up the contact with that low-life Gascon boy.

By the time Cumberland was finished grilling Eugenia, she

was too done in to think straight. Still, she knew one thing. She wasn't going to break down crying.

When she heard footsteps hurrying toward her, she looked up to see Rafe crossing the street.

"I thought you'd left."

"I figured you could use a ride home."

Cumberland must have grilled him too, but he seemed none the worse for wear. Just for a moment, she leaned into his strength, and his arm slipped lower, holding her against his side.

"You look worn out."

"I am."

"I'm sure the bastard gave you a hard time."

"How do you know?"

"I've met him before."

"He started off by quizzing me about the food I served. Then he basically told me I was crazy for having the voodoo ceremony in the first place."

"Too bad you can't get Calista to put a hex on him."

Despite everything, she laughed. "You're kidding, right?

"Yeah. Well, only partly. It would be convenient if she could work some magic and get him off our backs."

"Do you think Cumberland made everybody else wish they hadn't come to Voodoo Night?"

"Probably not. But he sees you as a tasty target."

She made a tsking sound. "What did he do to you?"

He shrugged. "Probably similar. He wanted to know where I was in relationship to Villars when he went down."

"Nice."

He cleared his throat. "Unfortunately, Villars and I have a history."

"What?"

He told her about his problem with the antique shop owner and the brooch.

And ended with, "Cumberland was the cop who showed up to scare the shit out of me."

She gasped. "Oh, Lord."

"I didn't take the jewelry, of course. It showed up in a drawer of an antique piece, but it got me and Cumberland off on the wrong foot." He sighed. "Too bad he decided to hustle over to your restaurant when he heard Villars had died."

"Right."

"And too bad Pete Grady didn't draw the case. He would have been more objective."

"Who's he?"

"A guy who went to high school with me. He's in the NOPD now."

"How do you know?"

"I did some checking around when Frank Decorah assigned me to this case."

She nodded, then realized suddenly that he was giving her the once-over.

"What?" she asked as she pushed her hair back from her face.

"You've had a hell of a day. And this is no place to be standing around having a discussion."

She looked back at the building. "You think they have microphones out here?"

"I wouldn't have been saying half of that stuff if I thought they were listening. But they do have surveillance cameras. Let me give you a ride home."

"I'm fine." She pulled herself up straighter, determined not to start being dependent on him—because he'd just be leaving again soon. Briskly, she headed away from his car. "I can get a cab."

He caught up with her. "No way."

The tone of his voice told her he wasn't going to let her go off on her own. Not now.

When they'd been teenagers, he'd never stepped over any boundary she'd set, although looking back, she knew he'd tempted her to do things she wouldn't have done with anyone else. Now their roles were reversed. He wasn't asking permission. He was telling her how things were, and she was having trouble rearranging her thinking.

There was a charged moment when she felt the tension crackling between them, and she knew for certain that the attraction they'd shared all those years ago hadn't gone away. It gave her some satisfaction knowing she could still affect him.

But she'd been thrown by the events of the past few hours. And although Rafe might look controlled, he had to be shaken by Cumberland's confrontational interrogation techniques. Maybe it was worse for him in a strange sort of way. She'd brought the situation on herself by having a questionable activity at her restaurant to earn a few extra bucks. Rafe had come here to try and catch the mugger ruining her business and gotten caught in a mess. A mess that had opened old animosities with the detective in charge of the case.

She reached to touch his arm. "I'm sorry."

"About what?"

"Sucking you into this. You signed up for one job, and it got out of hand real quick."

"I'm glad I was there."

The conviction in his voice warmed her.

"So was I," she admitted.

"Let's get in the car."

As she let him lead her across the street, she could feel her heart pounding.

When he opened the passenger door, she got in and leaned back against the seat, closing her eyes for a moment.

Her head snapped toward him as he got in beside her. She felt like she had lost her moorings—not just since Villars had keeled over, but since she'd looked up and seen Rafe Gascon standing in her restaurant.

And maybe it would help if he could answer a question that had haunted her for years.

She heard words escape her mouth before she had time to think about the consequences.

"Rafe, why did you walk away from me eight years ago?"

At first she was greeted with heavy silence. When he finally spoke, his voice was low and controlled. "I wasn't the one who walked away."

"That's not how I remember it. You left town."

"Because I had no future here. We both knew that."

"But . . ."

He cut her off before she could finish. "It doesn't matter now."

"Why not?"

"What really matters is that it was never going to work out for us."

"Why not?" she asked again.

"We were from two different worlds, and nothing's changed, chérie."

He'd never called her that before, and she didn't think he meant it as an endearment now. The assumption was reinforced by his blunt assessment, even though it was clear, from the moment they'd set eyes on each other, that there was still something between them. In her present state, that was too much to take, and she didn't want him to see the film of tears that suddenly clouded her vision.

Lowering her head, she reached for the door handle. He caught her hand and stopped her. When she tried to wrench away, he held her in place.

"I'm sorry. Neither one of us is in good enough shape for anything besides going home and going to bed."

Rafe stopped short, the words hanging in the air between them as he realized how that must sound. Was that what you called a Freudian slip? When you accidentally said what you were really thinking?

He chose to refocus the conversation. "Both of us have to stay cool. I think Cumberland enjoyed having us in his power, so to speak. For different reasons, of course. You can deny it, but you *are* New Orleans gentry, and he likes it that you're in trouble. With me, it's the old animosity surfacing.

My guess is that he would have loved it if I'd assaulted him, but I didn't take the bait."

"Oh Lord."

"So let's get the hell out of here."

Without waiting for an answer, he started the car and drove a few yards down the block, then saw that she wasn't wearing her seat belt. He could have told her to buckle up. Instead, after checking the rearview mirror, he stopped and reached across her to buckle the belt. The brush of his arm across her middle sent a small jolt of fire through him, and he drew his hand back quickly. It had been a test, and he'd failed it. Or maybe he'd passed it. He was too tired to puzzle it out. All he knew was that despite what he'd said about their being wrong for each other, there was no denying the sexual pull that still bound them.

Again he searched for a distraction and asked, "How come you live above the restaurant?"

"First, it shortens the commute. Second, it saves money."

He ignored the first part and asked "What about the Beaumont fortune? Or your mom's mansion?"

"There is no fortune. Neither of my parents understood frugality. And since my dad died five years ago, my mother has lived on her investment income, which has gone down because she dipped into too much of her principal to support her lifestyle. I did inherit some money from my grandfather, but it all went to equip the restaurant. Until those muggings, I was doing pretty well. Now I don't know what's going to happen. And for your information, I have no interest in living with my mother. She and I never got along real well. It was a relief to escape her constant criticism."

"I can relate to that."

"Your dad was hard on you."

"He didn't have a very happy life. His wife died young, and he was left with a kid to raise on his own—without a steady source of income."

"But he was good at his job."

"Damn good, but he couldn't always get work."

"I didn't know that."

"I didn't broadcast it. I wasn't proud of our lifestyle."

Eugenia slid him a glance, but he said nothing more, which gave her time to think about what his life must have been like. He hadn't talked a lot about it when they'd been teenagers, probably because the two of them had joined together in a kind of fantasy world that had to shatter eventually.

She cast him a sidelong glance and said, "You know a lot about me. Like where I live."

"I make it my business to know a lot about anybody when I'm assigned to work with them. And in this case, it was relevant, since you live in the area where your patrons were attacked."

"I guess."

"You don't have to guess; it's my job," he snapped.

She was sorry she'd challenged him. Since she'd come out of the police station, everything they said to each other seemed to lead to a confrontation or a subject one or the other of them didn't want to pursue. Too bad she wasn't in any kind of shape to keep her reactions normal. If she knew what normal was anymore.

He drove slowly after turning onto Dunlop Street, and she knew he was looking for muggers—which was what she'd hired him to do in the first place.

"The apartment door is in the courtyard."

"I'll go with you."

No use protesting that she didn't need him to walk her to her door. Instead she waited while he pulled up in the alley parking space from which she could walk to her patio and the back door of the restaurant.

When she saw the yellow crime-scene tape across the door, she sucked in a sharp breath.

"I didn't think of that," she murmured. "I guess nobody can go inside."

"At least for a few days."

They trooped past her secondhand wicker patio furniture, potted tropical plants and the angel statue she'd picked up at a garden center. She'd given the outdoor space an air of charm that usually made her smile. On Sunday mornings and warm nights when she wasn't working, she liked to sit out here, decompressing and dreaming up recipes she wanted to try. If this had been an ordinary evening, that's where she might have ended up. But nothing had turned out to be ordinary—starting with Rafe's walking in the door. The Villars death, Cumberland arriving and the ordeal at the police station.

And now there was the awkward moment of saying good night to Rafe.

"Are you going to be all right?" he asked.

"Yes." She tried to sound convincing, but probably they both knew she was lying.

"I'll talk to you after I meet with Pete," he said.

"In the morning?"

"Yes."

"I'm going with you."

She waited with her heart pounding. He could say "No."

Instead he answered with a brusque nod. "Okay. I'll pick you up at six."

As soon as Rafe turned and left, Eugenia unlocked her door and walked slowly up the steps. So far, she'd managed to hold herself together. Now that she was alone, she didn't have to pretend to anyone else that she was doing okay. As she stood before her door, she started to shake so hard that she could hardly get the key into the lock.

She finally did it, then walked inside on wobbly legs. She got no farther than the sofa, where she sat down heavily and managed to kick off her shoes.

Raising her head, she looked around at her mismatched furnishings, a combination of family heirlooms and bargain finds. She'd enjoyed decorating the apartment, putting her own touch to the living space. This place had been a haven for her. Now she felt like her world had been turned upside down.

She'd been a fool to get involved with Calista. And she'd been a fool to think that she was over Rafe Gascon. The moment she'd set eyes on him, she'd known that the old feelings hadn't gone away.

But she had no idea where that left them.

She threw her head back, trying to relax without much success. Finally she forced herself to get up, walk down the hall to the bathroom and start getting ready for bed. She took off the dress she'd been wearing and hung it up, thinking that after the day's activities, it needed a trip to the cleaner. Once she'd taken off her bra, she pulled out one of the extra-long tee shirts that she liked to sleep in. After washing her face and brushing her teeth, she finally crawled into bed and closed her eyes. But every nerve in her body was still humming, and as she lay in the darkened bedroom, she thought she heard a noise outside.

Leaving the lights off, she sat up and strained her ears. It sounded like someone was definitely out there, prowling around in the alley. Was Rafe back, or what?

She wanted to open her door and call his name, but she knew that wasn't such a good idea. Logically, it couldn't be Rafe. Why would he come back after half an hour? Whoever was outside was being stealthy, trying not to make any noise. As she listened, she thought he'd moved from the alley to the patio.

She tiptoed into the living room, dug her cell phone out of her purse, and started pressing numbers. Not the cops. They hadn't done her any good so far. Instead she called Rafe.

CHAPTER FOUR

It had been a hell of a day, Rafe thought as he crossed the bedroom in his B&B. He had just kicked off his shoes and put his gun on the bedside table when his cell phone rang.

He unclipped it from the holster on his belt and looked at the number. It wasn't familiar, and he wondered who was calling him at midnight. Not one of the people from the restaurant because he hadn't given them his number.

"Hello?"

"Rafe."

It was Eugenia, and the way she said his name made his breath catch.

"I'm sorry to call you—after you just left."

"What's wrong?"

"I think there's someone sneaking around outside my apartment."

"I'll be right there." He pulled his shoes on again, put his gun back into the waistband of his slacks and went back to his parking space. A couple of minutes after he'd gotten into his room, he was heading back toward Eugenia's apartment. "Keep the phone on so we don't lose touch."

"Yes. Thanks."

He kept her talking, hoping that would reassure her, and glad for the innovation of modern technology. "If they break in, hang up and call 911."

She sucked in a breath, then answered, "Okay."

"Do you hear anything else?"

"I don't think so."

"Is your outside light on?"

"Yes."

A few minutes later he glided to a stop at the curb out front.

"I'm outside now."

"Do you see anyone?"

"Not yet. And I'm going to stop talking you."

"Right."

He entered her patio and started for Eugenia's door.

There was something lying on the mat, something dark and nasty looking. In the dim light, he couldn't get a clear look at it, but he saw chicken feathers sticking out from the sides. A needle crowned the top, and other unsavory things added to the yucky effect. It appeared to be a voodoo charm.

He was so focused on it that he wasn't aware of someone behind him. And by the time he figured out that he wasn't alone on the patio, it was already too late.

Something clanked onto the back of Rafe's head, and he went down. The next thing he knew, Eugenia was bending over him and calling his name.

"Rafe?"

"Um."

She was beside him on the cold concrete, her breasts brushing his chest. He wanted to reach up and cup one, but a light was in his eyes, making his head hurt.

"Rafe?" she said again, "Are you all right?"

"Yeah," he answered automatically.

"You said to keep the phone on, and I heard you make a sound like you were hurt."

"Did I?"

"Yes."

He focused on her touch as one of her palms stroked his cheek, a very pleasant sensation. He wanted to enjoy that tender touch for another few moments, but something was nagging at him.

"The gris-gris," he muttered.

"The voodoo charm?"

"You saw it?"

"Yes."

"I was looking at it when someone hit me." He thought for a moment. "It wasn't there when I brought you home."

"I guess whoever was sneaking around outside must have left it. It's still there."

He fought to keep his thoughts coherent. "Go get a plastic bag and put it inside. Don't touch it. Pick it up with a plastic fork or something."

"I can't just leave you here."

"I'll be fine." When she stayed where she was, he said, "Go on. The sooner you take care of it, the sooner we can both go inside."

She made a sound of distress, but she did as he asked.

As she hurried away, he waited a moment, then tried to push himself up. He was rewarded with a jolt of pain in his head, but he gritted his teeth and sat up. No way was she going to come back and find him still lying on the pavement.

It seemed like she was gone for a long time, then finally she was back. He saw that she was wearing a long tee shirt over faded jeans.

"The gris-gris is in a plastic bag. I put it inside the door. On the steps."

"Okay. Good."

She came down beside him again, her voice concerned.

"Were you unconscious?"

"No." Maybe for a second, but he wasn't going to tell her that.

The headache was his only real problem. Everything else seemed to be working fine.

"You should have stayed inside," he said.

"You mean when you got hit? What was I supposed to do —leave you lying out here?"

"I would have made it into your apartment." He cleared his throat. "I don't suppose you saw who hit me?"

"No. Sorry."

"Too bad I was so focused on the gris-gris that I didn't see him."

"It was a man?"

"I'm just guessing—from the direction of the blow. It would have been a pretty tall woman."

Figuring he might as well get it over with, he tried to stand up and fought another stab of pain.

"Rafe!"

Gingerly, he touched the back of his head. "Shit."

In the next second, the flashlight beam swung around, illuminating the sticky red stuff he hadn't wanted her to see.

"You're bleeding," she gasped.

"It's not serious," he answered automatically.

When another very bad thought made its way into his fogged brain, he cursed again.

"What?"

"My weapon."

"I found it. Next to you. You had it when you were here earlier?"

"Yeah. I checked it at the police station. Then got it back."

"It's right here."

He thanked the voodoo gods for small favors. All he needed was to have a gun registered in his name involved in a crime in the city. That would have detective Cumberland dancing around the station house.

After checking the safety and jamming the piece into the waistband of his slacks, he let Eugenia help him up. Slowly they crossed the patio together. Inside the stairwell, she paused to get the bag with the gris-gris, then helped him the rest of the way upstairs.

She dropped the charm onto the coffee table.

He eyed the nasty looking calling card. "Somebody left that to scare you."

"We can deal with it later. Right now, we have to take care of your head."

"First, lock the door."

"Right."

"And close the blinds. Do you always keep them open at night?"

"Not in the bedroom."

He looked around her apartment while she complied, seeing a charming combination of what he judged were family pieces and flea market finds. He wanted to drop onto the three-cushion couch, but getting blood on it was a bad idea, so he wove his way down the hall, looking for the bathroom. When he found it, he closed the lid on the toilet seat and sat down.

Eugenia came in behind him.

"That gris-gris changes things," he said.

"I guess."

"It isn't exactly a housewarming gift. It's a very pointed warning. I don't like it."

"Maybe somebody's just trying to scare me," she murmured, obviously struggling to hold her voice steady.

"What's their motive?"

"What if someone who was at the ceremony is mad at me?"

"You mean like Calista?" He thought for a moment. "It would be dumb of her to be so obvious. But it could be someone else who thinks it can actually do you harm."

She didn't protest that the thing was harmless. Instead she said, "I have to turn on the light."

He shut his eyes, then opened them enough to look at her through lowered lashes as she leaned over him to check his head. This time, one of her breasts was practically in his face, and she wasn't wearing a bra. He could see the dark circle of the nipple right at eye level and felt his heart rate accelerate.

What would she do if he lifted his hand to touch her?

Before he could find out, her arm brushed the top of his head, and a stab of pain reminded him why she was so close.

"Rafe, I'm sorry," she murmured when he winced. "I was trying to see your wound."

"I know. How is it?"

"I can't tell yet. I have to wash it off."

She got a washcloth from the linen closet, then wet it with warm water and dabbed carefully at his scalp.

"Well?"

"A lump and a small gash. I think you need stitches. Probably you should go to the emergency room."

"Is it still bleeding?"

"It wasn't—until I washed it."

"It will crust over again. Forget the stitches. I'm not going to waste hours at the hospital when whoever that was could come back. Just put some antiseptic on the cut."

She opened the medicine cabinet. "I only have alcohol."

"Go for it."

"It will sting."

"My punishment for letting the guy brain me."

He gritted his teeth at the sting of the alcohol. When she

finished, she drew back and met his eyes. "You should get medical attention," she tried again.

"I'm tough." To prove it, he stood up, waited a moment to make sure he was steady on his feet, then walked down the hall to the living room where he sat down on the sofa and looked at the voodoo charm.

She followed him down the hall and turned on a low light in the corner of the room before sitting down in one of the chairs opposite him.

———————

He gestured toward the gris-gris. "I'd like to find out if that thing is a practical joke—or if it's meant to harm you."

"How?"

"By seeing if I can go back to when it was made."

"You're not in any kind of shape for that."

Maybe she was right, but he wasn't going to wimp out now. Leaning forward, he reached out and grabbed the bag, pressing his fingers through the plastic and lightly squeezing the charm inside, avoiding the needle. It wasn't direct contact, but it was enough. Immediately, the room swam around him and disappeared. He was somewhere else. A few hours ago when he'd touched the knife, he'd gone to the bayou. This time he was in a house. Nicely furnished. He saw an Oriental rug on the floor, overstuffed furniture. A lamp was on in the corner, but it was the only source of light. Was he going back to another voodoo ceremony?

He saw his hands. A man's hands, encased in surgical gloves.

A collection of objects was spread out on the low table in front of him. Chicken feathers. Dried cloves. Dried garlic. A smelly crawfish claw. A couple of toothpicks. A needle. What looked like mustard but might not be. A broken knife blade. A small wad of paper towel. The man leaned down and spit on the towel, then crumpled it up and plopped spittle onto what looked like a blob of dark putty.

He moved his hand through the objects on the table, picking up pieces and turning them one way and the other. Pulling some down and picking up others, he pressed them into the base material.

Rafe had no idea who was fashioning the thing. Or where the room was. He wasn't in his own body, and he had only minimal control of the situation. For example, he couldn't walk out of the room. He had to stay where the man was.

But could he stand up for a better view of the interior space? When he started to try it, he pitched to the side, falling against the corner of a desk. Pain seared into his side where the horizontal surface gouged him.

A voice came to him from far away. "Rafe, are you all right, Rafe?"

Was he?

His eyes blinked open, and he focused on Eugenia who had crossed the room and was sitting beside him on the sofa. When he realized he was slumped over, he straightened up.

"Are you all right," she asked again, her voice urgent as she closed her hand over his shoulder.

"Yes."

"What happened?"

"I wanted to get an impression of whoever made that thing."

"And you did?"

"Yeah. But not enough."

"What does that mean?"

"I saw a room, but it was mostly dark."

"A cabin? Something in town?"

"In town, I'm pretty sure. It was nicely furnished. I remember an Oriental rug."

"Could you identify the pattern?"

He laughed. "I'm not that into decor. I saw someone putting the charm together, but I don't know who it was."

"Man or woman?"

"A man, I'm pretty sure."

She stroked his shoulder. "You shouldn't have done that."

"It's part of my job."

"What do you mean?"

"It's why Frank Decorah sent me—and not somebody else. He knows I can enter a scene generated by things I touch. He thought it might help me figure out who's behind the muggings."

"Has it helped?"

He answered with another laugh—this one more hollow. "With this case? Not so far."

After Rafe had figured out that touching things could give him impressions of the object's owner, he'd played around with it, trying to figure out who had been doing what. Once he'd stumbled into a scene where one of his friends had been bent on seduction in the backseat of a car. Another time he'd seen his father sitting alone in his room, holding a picture of his mother. That had cured him of making a game of eavesdropping on people. And since beginning his investigative career, the skill had turned into serious business.

He moved on the sofa and winced.

"What?"

"I hit my side against a desk."

"When?"

"When I was . . . away."

"You can get hurt in one of those visions?"

"Yeah."

"So now you've gotten hurt twice in less than two hours. I've made a mess of this, haven't I?" she said suddenly.

"What do you mean?"

"I never should have gotten sucked into letting Calista hold a voodoo service at Chez Eugenia."

"Whose idea was it?"

She dragged in a breath and let it out. "Calista's."

"Why did she want to do it?"

"She said it gave her access to a clientele she wouldn't have otherwise met. Which makes sense. She seemed to be trying to expand her customer base."

Glad to take the focus of the conversation off himself, he asked, "How did you meet *her*?"

"At a big reception I was catering out at one of the plantations along the river. They're open to tourists during the day, and at night they can be rented for private functions. We were both hired help, and we got to talking. Then she suggested we meet for coffee sometime soon. She called to arrange it, and I agreed. I guess she had already started thinking about using my restaurant as a venue for holding a service."

"Nice."

"It worked out for me, too. It was a fusion of New Orleans cultures, and that made it interesting. She called some of the local publications, and we got an article about the first event."

"I saw it—in one of the tourist magazines."

"Right."

"You're a good cook; you don't need tricks to get customers."

"How do you know I'm a good cook?"

"I remember your chocolate chip cookies—and your pecan pie," he said, hearing his voice thicken.

"Kid stuff."

"You had the knack."

"Okay, I know I have the knack. More than that, I know I'm good at thinking up interesting flavor combinations. But when you're first starting out, every little bit of advertising helps. There are a lot of great restaurants in the Big Easy. Anything I could do to draw in customers was a plus. If someone came to a voodoo performance on a whim and liked my food, they might come back. And it also attracted people from out of town. But it turned out to be a bad idea." She laughed. "As soon as I saw a live chicken in a cage, I cringed."

He asked one of the questions that had been bugging him. "Was she going to kill it?"

"Not in the restaurant. Maybe she does out in the bayou."

He sat forward. "Why did you say—the bayou?"

She shrugged. "I was just picturing her there, in a clearing with a lot of followers."

He nodded. "Didn't you read up on voodoo before you agreed?"

"Yes. But, like I said, I didn't think she was going to go that far in a restaurant in the French Quarter."

"Well, don't beat yourself up over it. You made a mistake, but you don't have to do it again."

Her voice rose. "A man is dead because of me."

"Not *because* of you. It's not your fault." He gave her a considering look. "Are you afraid of Calista?"

She clenched and unclenched her fists. "Yes," she whispered.

"Why?"

"She has abilities other people don't."

"You believe that?"

"I've seen things happen. Someone will come into money. Or lose it. Or . . ." she lifted one shoulder. "Or they might end up in the hospital."

"You think she has the power to do that?"

"I'd be foolish not to act as though I did. You said I had the touch as a cook. It's like that with Calista and voodoo."

"Do you think she killed Villars?"

"I don't know. I mean, what would be her motive?"

"He could have done something to her—something you don't know about."

"It was a pretty public forum. Which means she'd be taking a big chance." She clenched her fists. "This whole situation keeps getting worse and worse."

"We'll figure it out. Did Calista ask who had made reservations?"

"Yes."

"Interesting. She asked each time?"

"Yes." She swallowed hard. "I feel like my life is spinning out of control," she said suddenly.

The distress in her voice tore at him. He gathered her close, turning her in his arms. As they stared at each other, he went very still, and it was the most natural thing in the world to take comfort to another level.

In unconscious invitation, Eugenia tipped her head to a more convenient angle, her lips parted.

She heard Rafe mutter something she couldn't quite catch. Perhaps it was, "I've been wanting to do this all evening."

Or was that what she wanted to hear?

Had the voodoo gods brought her soul mate back to her after all these years?

All she knew was that she had longed to feel his lips on hers—since when? Not when he'd first walked into Chez Eugenia. She'd been too startled then, but she'd quickly started imagining it.

She wasn't disappointed in the reality. The first mouth-to-mouth contact was like a jolt of sensation, more than she had dared to imagine.

It had been eight years since she'd felt this surge of natural electricity with anyone. She'd been married to another man and divorced. Yet those two years with Richard Delaney were wiped away as though they had never happened. At this moment in time, she knew only the wonderful taste of Rafe Gascon, the taste of man and animal awareness tinged with the same desperation she felt. The last time he'd kissed her, he'd been a teenager saying good bye. And even though he'd known exactly what he was doing, it had been a boy's kiss. Now he was all grown up into a very formidable male. She felt the strength of his arms, the heat of his body as he gathered her close.

He made a deep possessive sound that claimed her as his own, overloading her senses and her mind, making the years they'd been apart disappear.

She had thought about him during those years, but her imagination hadn't matched reality.

Perhaps long ago she'd intimidated him because she was Miss Debutante, and he was the son of the family handyman. Now he had taken charge of the kiss—taken charge of her. When he picked her up and settled her in his lap, she made a needy sound and pressed her breasts against his chest. They had been this close before. Closer. He could make her body respond as no other man ever could. He knew what she liked and what would bring her to climax—with his hands and mouth because she had set the rules. Or avoiding pregnancy was one time when she'd listened to her mother. "If that boy gets you in real trouble, it's your own fault."

Tonight she longed to know what making love with him would be like. Not the way they'd played around as kids. And she wasn't sure what would have happened if he hadn't suddenly and abruptly ended the kiss.

He set her back onto the sofa, and they sat in silence for long moments.

"I'm sorry," she said.

"About getting close to me again?"

"No. About kissing you when you just got hit over the head."

He kept his gaze on her. "Thanks for reminding me why I'm here. Who are your enemies?"

CHAPTER FIVE

"You kiss me—and that makes you think of enemies?"

"I'm getting back to business."

She answered with a reluctant nod. She knew he'd responded to her. Now he was deliberately throwing cold water on the heat between them.

She turned her palm up in a helpless gesture. "I didn't think I had any enemies. Well—there's that guy who tried to run out the door. You stopped him, but I could see he was angry with both of us. And Cumberland said he was an illegal alien."

"You know his name?"

"I'll have to get it from Calista."

"She has reason to be mad at you, too. You're obviously not inviting her back. And you got her noticed by a very nasty cop."

"All that happened after Villars death."

"True. But the gris-gris wasn't here earlier."

"You don't think Calista left it, do you?"

"I guess that's too obvious."

"Then who?"

"Like I said, who are your enemies?"

"Well the woman down the street who owns a beauty shop called Headliner was never very friendly. Then when the muggings started, she began giving me dirty looks—like I was making the street unsafe."

"And how is that connected to you specifically?"

"It never happened until I got Chez Eugenia started. And the people who were mugged were my customers."

"And it didn't start until after you got successful."

"Yes."

"What's her name?"

"Mrs. Houston. She didn't tell me her first name."

"Friendly of her." He wrote it down before asking, "Who else?"

She took her bottom lip between her teeth, then released it. "I guess I should mention my cousin Bennett. He . . . uh . . . was angry that my restaurant was doing better than his. At Thanksgiving, he'd had too much to drink, and he got me in a corner and threatened to put me out of business."

"Oh yeah."

"He was upset. I don't think he meant it."

Rafe pulled out his notepad. "His last name is Beaumont?"

"Yes."

"What's his address? Home and restaurant."

She gave them to him, then asked, "What are you going to do?"

"Have a chat with him. And tomorrow we can talk to

Calista—after we talk to Pete Grady. But let's get back to the enemies list."

"A nice way to put it. I'm not Richard Nixon."

"Hardly. Did a patron ever threaten you?"

"For what?"

"Charging too much for food he didn't like."

"No."

"What about your staff? Did you fire anyone who might resent it?"

She thought for a moment. "I did fire a kid who was washing dishes for me. But he was working over summer vacation. He's out of town at college."

"Okay. If you think of anyone else, tell me."

Eugenia gave him a considering look. "You look done in."

"Thanks."

"You did get hit on the head."

"And I don't want to leave you alone for the rest of the night."

"You don't think the person who left the gris-gris will come back, do you?"

"I hope not, but I'd rather be here if he does."

"I've only got one bed," she said, then flushed as she thought about how that must sound.

"The sofa's fine," he answered easily.

"It's not that comfortable. And you need to sleep. You can take the bed."

"I'm not kicking you out of your room."

The statement hung in the air between them.

Calista's eyes narrowed as she looked at the tall man with coffee-colored skin and high cheekbones who stood in front of her with his head bowed. He was from the Islands, with that soft, lilting accent that she liked so much, but he probably had as much white blood as African. His heritage had combined very nicely to give him a tall, broad-shouldered body and pleasing features. A narrow nose. Sensual lips. Light-colored eyes and the kind of penis that she liked. Not overly long but nice and thick.

His name was Justin. She'd hired him six months ago to be her chief drummer, and he'd done well at that job. But she'd quickly found that he had other attractions.

Now he had added to her problems.

Before the cops had taken them in for questioning, she'd told him to meet her back at her house in Gentilly.

She was angry with Justin, but she knew how to use that anger to her advantage tonight. And tomorrow she'd face whatever else was coming her way from the fiasco at Chez Eugenia.

"You told me Lorenzo was okay," she said in an accusing voice.

"I thought he was," he answered in his soft island accent. "You needed another drummer on short notice. I knew he could handle the assignment."

"You didn't know he was illegal?"

"I . . ."

"You suspected."

He answered with a small nod. "But I didn't know someone was going to die tonight."

"Are you sure?"

His face took on a look of outrage. "What do you mean? Of course I'm sure."

"But you brought trouble to me. Where is Lorenzo now?"

"He's gone."

"Where?"

He shrugged. "Away from the cops."

"And you are here. You must be punished."

"As you wish."

"Take off your clothes. Fold them neatly and lay them on the table."

He kept his gaze fixed somewhere over her shoulder as he pulled off his tee shirt and folded it before laying it on the table beside him. Then he did the same with his jeans and shorts.

When he turned back to her, she saw that he was aroused.

"Precede me down the hall. You know which room."

Again he did as she ordered. She could feel her excitement rising as she stepped into what might have been a spare bedroom, unless you looked carefully. In one corner was a basket of artificial flowers hanging from the ceiling, secured by a very sturdy chain.

"Take down the flowers," she said.

He did as instructed, exposing a metal hook.

"Hold out your hands."

Again he followed her bidding and she opened the antique armoire to his right, taking out leather cuffs attached to a strap. She looped the strap over the hook, then attached the cuffs to his hands so that he was secured with his back to her and his hands over his head.

He was her captive now, and she stroked her nails over his broad back, then down to his butt, kneading the hard muscles before reaching around him, clasping her hand around his cock, squeezing, dragging a moan from him.

"If you come before I give you permission, you will be sorry," she warned.

He said nothing, only stood rigidly in place while she took off her gown, draping it over a wooden chair before returning to her captive. She was as naked as he, and she undulated against him, rubbing her breasts against his back and her clit against his butt, feeding her own arousal as she reached to lightly stroke his cock, feeling it jump in her hand.

She went back to the armoire and examined the implements laid neatly on shelves, considering the advantages of each. Finally she decided she wanted to see the short welts on his skin made by a riding crop.

After selecting the implement, she returned to Justin. Raising her arm, she brought the lash down on his back, hard enough to sting. She gave him more blows, working her way down to his buttocks, hearing him groan as she punished him, knowing he was responding to the pain with excitement.

She was panting when she had finished, and she heard his breath in her ears as she unfastened the cuffs so he could bring his hands down.

His face was flushed. His body quivering.

She went to a rounded wooden chair with low arms and sat down, draping her legs over the arms and thrusting her hot, wet pussy toward him.

"Eat me," she commanded.

He knelt in front of her, bending his head and expertly using his tongue and lips to bring her to a rocketing climax.

And only when she had been satisfied once did she lie down on the bed at the side of the room. Spreading her legs again, she looked up at him. Making him wait, she licked her lips and played with her nipples as she watched him.

When she thought he might go up in flames kneeling there, she said, "You may fuck me now. And you may let yourself come."

With a sound deep in his throat, he climbed to his feet and came down on the bed, covering her body with his, thrusting into her, bringing her to another enormous climax and then letting himself go.

He held her for a moment, daring to kiss her cheek.

"You're heavy."

He moved off of her, lying on the bed, breathing hard.

"You have good control."

"For you."

"Does your back hurt?" she asked.

"Yes."

"You deserve it."

"Yes."

"And more."

She rose from the bed, pulling up the straps that hung below the spread at the sides.

"Lie on your back."

When he had complied, she secured his wrists and ankles, then reached for his cock, caressing him, bringing him to a full erection again. She had had a hell of a night, and she needed to relax.

She ran her hand over the smooth skin of his chest. Then, lighting a candle, she brought it over and tipped it sideways so that the hot wax fell between his nipples, then directly on one of them. He winced but said nothing, and she moved the candle lower, dripping wax onto his abdomen, watching his muscles jump.

She had selected him for her retinue because he was an excellent drummer, and she had sensed that he would play the role of her slave. But he could reverse the roles. If she wanted, he could bring her the pain that she sometimes craved.

"I have a queen-sized bed. It will be big enough for both of us."

Rafe stared at her, wondering how much sleep he was going to get.

"I'll put out a towel and washcloth for you."

"Okay," he answered, hearing the thickened quality of his voice.

So much had changed since he'd last seen Eugenia Beaumont.

He'd left New Orleans and made a good life for himself, and he'd told himself a million times that he was better off without a woman who would never understand the problems of a working stiff. He'd thought it was true—until he'd seen Eugenia looking just as beautiful and desirable as he remembered. And seen the life she'd chosen for herself—a life that included a lot of hard work and sacrifice.

She could still be married to that rich guy, living in a fancy house with expensive furnishings, and spending her time playing golf and being on charity committees. Instead she was doing everything she could to make her restaurant a success. He could see that she wasn't spending much on furnishing her apartment, although he loved the effect she'd created.

The restaurant location was another clue to the state of her finances. It was at the extreme edge of the French Quarter, beyond the French Market. Not exactly the best part of town. No wonder two of her patrons had been mugged. Or was that connected with this current case? Was Villars' death an attack on Eugenia?

His mind returned to the kiss that should never have happened. He could have taken it a lot further and made love with her, but he'd done the right thing and stopped before they'd gone too far. Too bad he was still in her apartment and headed for her bed.

CHAPTER SIX

Rafe used the bathroom, then walked slowly into the bedroom. Eugenia was already in bed, way over to the far side, and he wondered if he could really lie next to her and get any sleep.

Determined to keep things professional, he eased onto the mattress beside her. He longed to reach for her, but he contented himself with slowly sliding his arm over until the backs of their hands touched.

Immediately he wanted more. How far could he push this? Probably all the way. But then he'd be where he'd been when he'd broken off the kiss.

Still, as he drifted off, he let a little fantasy curl through his brain. A fantasy in which she turned to him in her sleep, and they ended up a tangle of bodies in the morning.

Sometime before sunrise Eugenia slept—then woke to sensations she hadn't experienced in a long time.

She was lying on her side, pressed against a very hard male body. An aroused male body, she realized.

When she heard Rafe swallow hard, she knew he'd figured out she was awake.

Through a screen of lashes, she saw that he was looking at her, his eyes bright and his skin slightly flushed. He said nothing, but one of his hands slid down her body, tracing the indentation of her waist, then cupping her hips and pulling her more tightly against himself.

She made a small sound that might have started as a protest, although she wasn't absolutely sure. She should move away. Too bad her body didn't seem to be in sync with good sense.

Closing her eyes again, she lowered her head to Rafe's shoulder, pressing her face against the soft fabric of his tee shirt, feeling his hot skin beneath.

She had started doing intimate things with Rafe Gascon when she'd been sixteen. And the only reason they'd stopped was that he'd left town. They'd never been in a bedroom together. But they'd brought an old mattress up to the loft in the garage—where they'd spent a lot of quality hours together, always alert to someone's discovering their clandestine meeting place. That was kid stuff. Now they were all grown up, and he was in her bed, his thoughts probably running along the same lines as hers.

She saw his hand move, felt it gently cup her breast, then stroke back and forth across the hardened tip. His touch made her blood heat.

"Lord, that's so good, chérie," he murmured.

"Yes." He'd never called her that until yesterday—when it had sounded like an insult. Now it was an endearment.

One of her arms was trapped between them. With her free hand she stroked along the curve of his hip and down his leg, wishing she felt naked skin instead of twill fabric.

He gathered her closer, his arms circling her body, his hands working their way down to her bottom. Rolling over, she pressed him to his back and heard him groan.

From pain, she realized, because she'd jammed his head against the pillow—which wasn't exactly a hard surface.

Her immediate thought was that someone should slap her upside the head. He'd been hurt last night outside her apartment, and here she was acting like he was perfectly all right.

She sprang away from him, then pushed herself off the bed.

"I'm sorry," she managed.

"Why?"

"Because it's obvious your head hurts from getting hit last night."

"You were always logical."

She wanted to protest that she wouldn't have gotten tangled up with him in the first place if she'd been logical, but she bit back the comment as unhelpful.

He sat up carefully, his movements slow and deliberate.

"You and I need to talk," she murmured.

"About what?"

"About us."

"There is no us," he said in a voice that told her the conversation had ended.

She wasn't going to let that slide by. "Then what were you doing a few minutes ago—amusing yourself with me?"

"No."

"Then what?"

"This isn't the time for a personal discussion."

"When is?"

"I wish I knew."

Was that progress or not?

He'd stayed here last night to protect her—after getting hurt. And she wasn't in such good shape herself. She didn't even know how she was supposed to behave with him. With her lips pressed together she turned her back on him and pulled clean underwear from her dresser, then found a tee shirt and jeans. Wadding the clothing into a ball, she headed for the bathroom, where she showered and dressed in record time.

When she came back, she thought Rafe had left, and she felt a terrible sense of loss. But what had she been thinking? That everything would magically be fine between them now that he was back in town?

She was adjusting to his absence when he walked back in the front door.

"Where were you?" she heard herself say.

"Getting the bag I keep in the car and checking outside."

"Did you find anything?"

"Just some of my blood."

That got her attention. She was feeling wounded because he'd rejected her. But really she should be thinking that getting coldcocked might have put him in a bad mood. He was obviously still in pain—and working hard not to show it. And the incident hadn't done his macho image any good.

"I'll be in better shape after I shower and change," he said.

Was that a roundabout way of apologizing?

Before she could decide, she was left standing in the living room staring after him.

While Rafe was in the bathroom, she made a pot of chicory-laced coffee, then called her staff and told them the restaurant would be closed for a few days and she'd let them know when she could reopen again. In some cases she left messages on answering machines.

Thankful that she kept her restaurant materials well organized, she opened the computer file with the menu and recipes from the night before and e-mailed them to Detective Cumberland.

By the time Rafe emerged from the bathroom, she was standing in front of the television set, watching the news. Which showed a picture of Chez Eugenia on the screen. The voice-over gave a breathless account of the voodoo ceremony and Martin Villars' death. Just when she thought the segment was over, the report went on to give a rehashing of the mugging incidents.

"That's just what I need," she muttered as she sensed Rafe standing in back of her. "I guess I don't have to worry about Cumberland closing me," she added. "Nobody will be coming, anyway."

Rafe moved up behind her and slid a comforting arm around her waist. "They'll come. First because they're curious. You'll get the same kind of tourists who attended the voodoo ceremony—looking for zombies.

She snorted.

"And you'll get the people who have liked your food all along. And then everybody will end up talking about your fabulous cuisine and forget about last night."

"You aren't just saying that?"

"It's the truth."

"Let's hope so."

She sighed, going back to the previous thought. "It looks like the dumbest thing I ever did was to let Calista talk me into using the restaurant."

"We don't always know the consequences of our choices."

Was there some hidden message in the words? Or should she simply stop second-guessing every exchange they had.

"I want to ask her some questions this morning," he said, his voice hard-edged. She flicked her gaze toward him. It sounded like he cared about helping her—not just because she'd hired Decorah Security to investigate the muggings. But there was no way to know for sure—not unless he was willing to open up about why he'd failed to keep his promise to her eight years ago.

When the phone rang, she snatched up the instrument.

"Eugenia, are you all right?"

She tightened her hand on the receiver. It was her mother, pretending to be worried about her.

"I'm fine."

"I just saw on TV that you were holding a voodoo ceremony at your restaurant last night, and someone died."

"Yes."

"I didn't know about anything like that. How long has this been going on?"

"This is the first death," she answered.

"Don't be smart with me, how long have you been exposing yourself to a dangerous element?"

"Nine months."

Her mother made a clucking sound. "Why didn't you call me last night so I wouldn't have to find out about it from the television?"

"It was late when I got back from the police station, and I didn't want to disturb you," she lied. Really, she hadn't even thought about her mother. She'd gotten herself out of the habit because a conversation with Mom was likely to end up being unpleasant—like now. Her mother hadn't understood why she hadn't wanted to get a normal college degree like all her friends and then settle down as the wife of a man who would make the rules for her. The way Richard Delaney had done, as it turned out. He'd seemed like he loved her. Then he'd put obstacles in the way of her having a career. Looking back, she should have known that would happen.

"I'm disturbed now," her mother was saying. She huffed out an exasperated breath. "You knew you were doing something very foolish by letting that voodoo woman use your premises."

Right. And she hadn't had the courtesy to run the idea by Mom and get a vote of no confidence. All she said was, "I'm sorry you think so."

"You shouldn't let that element anywhere near your place of business."

"Right, Mom," she answered, because she'd learned long ago that the best way to deal with her mother was to go along with what she was saying—at least while she was saying it. "I'll take care of it."

"Eugenia . . ."

"Yes?"

"I'm only trying to help. You know I always have your best interests in mind."

"Of course," she answered remembering all the times when Mom thought her best interests and her own ideas about that were in strong conflict.

"Have the police found out what killed that poor man?"

"If they have, they haven't shared it with me."

When she finally hung up, she found Rafe watching her.

"Your mom?"

"Yes."

"She always was . . ." he raised one shoulder.

"Difficult," Eugenia finished for him. "And very sure she knows what's best. I hate it that in this case, she was right."

"Will you be okay while I go talk to Pete?"

"Did you forget I want to go with you?"

She saw him start to object, then must have thought better of trying to set the rules, particularly in light of the conversation he'd just heard her half of. Still, he did say, "It's probably going to be a more productive meeting if I go alone."

"You may think so, but I don't agree. I hired Decorah Security to investigate the muggings. I don't want to be shut out of information."

He waited a beat, obviously weighing alternatives. "Okay."

"Thanks," she answered, relieved that they weren't going to have an argument, because she wasn't up for any more drama this morning.

As they finished their preparations, he asked, "Something I'm curious about. How did you pick Decorah Security?"

She shrugged. "I looked online and I saw some of the cases the agency had handled. I guess I liked the way you all came across."

He answered with a nod.

"Did the owner—Frank Decorah—know about your . . . I don't know what to call it. "Your special ability when he hired you?"

"Yes."

"And he liked that?"

"Yes. He's got other agents who have something extra."

"Like what?"

"Probably we shouldn't talk about the other guys."

"Right."

By six forty-five, they were out of the apartment. As she put a notice on the front door of the restaurant saying she'd be open again soon, she tried to ignore the curious stares of some of the people who'd seen the police commotion and the news reports. When she spotted the tall, willowy figure of Mrs. Houston from the beauty shop, pushing her way toward the front of the crowd, she sucked in a breath. The woman's blond hair was beautifully arranged, but her black dress did nothing to enliven her dour face.

Rafe followed her gaze. "That's the woman who doesn't like it that you moved in?"

"Yes."

Mrs. Houston stepped into Eugenia's path, blocking her escape route as she said, "I warned you that voodoo stuff was bad news."

"I'm sorry you feel that way," she answered pleasantly, thinking that Mrs. Houston and her mom were on the same wavelength. Had they cooked up something together to turn people away from the restaurant? And it had gotten out of hand?

Even as the thought formed, she dismissed it.

"And that voodoo death has given the whole neighborhood a bad name. I guess now you'll think twice about repeating the mistake."

"It wasn't a voodoo death."

"What was it?"

"We don't know."

"Then it could have been."

Before she could argue with the woman further, Rafe stepped between them.

"Ms. Beaumont has some business to attend to this morning. I'm sure she'd be happy to talk to you another time," he said.

"Glad to hear it. And who are you? Besides the guy who spent the night with her last night?"

CHAPTER SEVEN

In the dead silence that followed, Rafe fought the urge to explain why he'd been in Eugenia's apartment overnight. Instead he took her arm. She let him lead her to the car and open the door, where she dropped like a stone into the passenger seat.

"So now as far as she's concerned, I'm a voodoo messenger of death and a slut," she muttered.

"Do you care?"

"I shouldn't."

Should he have spent the night, he wondered. The answer was the same as it had been the night before. If he hadn't been there, the person who'd attacked him could have come upstairs and gone after Eugenia.

He slid her a quick glance. She was sitting rigidly in her seat, staring straight ahead. He wanted to reach out and lay his hand over hers. He wanted to say he was sorry her nosy neighbor was keeping tabs on her. And he wanted to say he was sorry the two of them couldn't figure out how to act around each other.

He cleared his throat. "What specifically has Mrs. Houston done before—that you know of?"

Eugenia clasped her hands in her lap. "Only let me know that I'm not welcome here."

"Do you think she'd take it to the next level?"

She'd been thinking something like that a few minutes earlier. "Like sneak around in the alley? To do what?"

"I don't know. Do you think she'd arrange to have your customers mugged?"

Her eyes widened. "Are you accusing her of that?"

"You know she's on the suspect list. And she was pretty hostile just now."

"Mostly she's a big talker. Or—I guess you could say she's been here a long time, and she thinks she knows what's good for this street."

"But would she do something illegal to get you to move?"

"I hope not. On the other hand, she probably saw you taking me home last night, and she could have been snooping around to find out what we were up to. When you showed up in the alley, she hit you and ran."

"That's possible."

She sighed. "But it's hard to picture her actually mounting an attack."

"Let's consider another suspect," he said.

"Who?"

"Your cousin."

"Why him?"

"Because in his eyes, you're a rival."

"Yes. But I wonder if he really thinks there's not room for both of us in New Orleans. I mean, the Brennan family has at least ten restaurants, and they all get along."

"They get along, as far as you know. They probably don't advertise their conflicts."

"You could be right."

"How well do you know Cousin Bennett?"

"We played together as kids. But we don't run in the same circles now. Like I said, the last time we saw each other was at Thanksgiving. We were never exactly friends."

"Where was that?"

"Another cousin's house."

"And you both brought food?"

She laughed. "I did. Cornbread stuffing, crawfish etouffee."

"For Thanksgiving?"

"This is New Orleans, after all."

"What did he bring?"

"Wine."

"And everyone praised your food."

"Yes."

She dragged in a breath and let it out. "He didn't cook. That's not his thing."

"I'm confused. How does he have a restaurant and not cook?"

"He hires a chef. He's been through three different ones

in four years. He gets into arguments with them about the cost of food."

"How does he think he's going to make it in a town with a very competitive restaurant scene?"

"He's got charm. He makes people feel welcome."

"Maybe that's not good enough."

"It could be—if he has the right person in the kitchen. There are tourists who don't know a lot about fine dining. They get a meal from him that's good enough. Or they can't get reservations at one of the top places, so they settle. Actually, I've gotten customers that way."

"And you know all this about him—how?"

"The foodie community here is like a small town. Word gets around. But the tourists don't hear the rumblings."

Rafe nodded. "It sounds like he's going about this completely differently from you."

She nodded.

"He's a couple years older than you are?"

"Yes."

"And he started before you?"

"Yes. He got a good deal on a restaurant, in an excellent location."

"He could afford it?"

"His part of the family was better with money."

"What else do you consider significant about him?"

"My mother likes him. She used to compare us unfavorably."

"Nice of her."

She laughed. "Mom has high standards. I didn't necessarily meet them."

He wanted to say, "Like hanging out with the handy-man's son." But he kept the comment to himself.

Eugenia had never been to Café LaBret and was interested to see it.

Rafe slowed as he approached the restaurant, which was on a side street off St. Charles. He found a parking space down the block, and they both walked back. The interior was a relentless homage to the fifties, with Formica and chrome fixtures and black and white vinyl tile on the floor. Instead of big flat-screen TVs with sports events, there were a couple of clunky old television sets showing I Love Lucy segments. You could eat at the counter or at one of the booths or tables in the back, and the waitresses all wore pink uniforms with white aprons.

When they walked in, Rafe nodded to a man who was already sitting at a table for two. He looked up, saw Eugenia and gave Rafe a questioning look. He answered with a small shrug.

As they walked back, Eugenia saw that his police detective friend was about Rafe's age, with light brown hair cut almost military short, blue eyes and a solid build. He was wearing a blue sports jacket and gray pants, an outfit considerably less grand than what Cumberland had worn the night before.

"Pete Grady, this is Eugenia Beaumont."

Although he obviously wasn't pleased to see her tagging

along, he said, "Nice to meet you—although I wish the circumstances were better."

She nodded. "Nice to meet you, too. I understand you're an old friend of Rafe's."

"Yeah, we got in trouble together back in the day."

He picked up his coffee cup and carried it from the smaller table to a nearby booth that could accommodate all of them. When he sat down, Rafe and Eugenia sat opposite him.

He gave Eugenia a considering look. "When Rafe and I arranged to get together, I didn't expect to see you here."

The blunt words made her realize that perhaps she'd made a mistake in insisting on coming along. Her presence definitely made this a business meeting.

"So are you here to make sure I'm not telling Rafe anything he doesn't want you to find out?"

"I guess you could talk on the phone for that."

The detective nodded. Shifting in his seat, he looked at Rafe. "What is it that you want—exactly?"

A middle-aged waitress with dyed yellow hair came over. "Coffee?"

"Yes, thanks," Rafe said. He picked up the menu and studied the selections.

"The blueberry pancakes are good," Pete said.

"Sold."

When the waitress came back with their coffee, they all ordered breakfast, with Eugenia opting for, "two eggs over with wheat toast and bacon."

Once they were alone again, Pete gave Rafe a questioning look.

"I was hoping you could keep me in the loop on the investigation," Rafe said.

The detective waited a beat before answering. "I could lose my job if anybody found out."

"Yeah," Rafe agreed.

Pete flicked his eyes toward Eugenia and then away, making her wish she hadn't crashed this party. There might be things Pete wouldn't risk telling Rafe in front of her that he'd say if the two men were alone

"Well, if there *is* anything you can share, I'd appreciate it," Rafe said.

The food came, and the men poured a liberal amount of syrup on their pancakes.

They discussed the case in a general way, with Rafe doing more of the talking, filling in his friend on what he'd observed so far. Probably Grady was thinking that she'd been stupid to get into the voodoo business. But nobody said it out loud.

Toward the end of the meal, the detective forked up a bite of pancakes, chewed and swallowed.

"Cumberland is bucking for a promotion," he said.

"Oh yeah?" Rafe answered.

"He thinks he's going to make deputy chief."

"Will he?"

"He's not well liked in the department." He glanced at Eugenia. "If he can crack a high-profile case, it would be another check in his column."

"And I'm high profile?"

"Not exactly. But Villars has been a power in the business community for years."

"So he'd have enemies."

"Undoubtedly."

"Do we know if any of them were at the ceremony last night?"

"Can you tell me who was there?" Grady asked.

Rafe got out his cell phone and went down the list of guests.

"Nobody rings a bell," the detective said. "But you might want to check out a guy named Sam Gunderson."

"Why?"

"He and Villars were both interested in a piece of property in the French Quarter."

"For what?"

"A boutique hotel. Gunderson got it, and Villars was angry."

"That would make Gunderson go after him?"

"Villars had some nasty stuff to say—like that Gunderson was planning to set up a high-class whorehouse."

"Nice" Rafe murmured. "Thanks for the tip. I'll check him out."

As soon as they were out of the restaurant, Eugenia said, "Sorry."

"About what?"

"Barging in."

"He was being circumspect, but he could help us out later. It's obvious he doesn't like Cumberland." He laughed. "Probably nobody likes Cumberland."

She switched topics and asked, "How are you feeling?"

"Okay."

"You only ate half your pancakes."

"Pancakes are filling."

"Then why did you order them?"

"I haven't had any in a long time. Are you going to grill me on my eating habits?"

"I'm concerned that you may have had a concussion last night, and you're not feeling one hundred percent today."

"Maybe not a hundred percent, but close."

They had reached the car. After they got in, she said, "Maybe we'll do better with Calista."

"I think she's also going to be reluctant to share anything significant, but we have to try."

He punched in the address, then headed back to the French Quarter, where he found a parking space on Chartres Street. As they walked back to the shop, Eugenia was very conscious of his hand dangling only a few inches from hers.

She'd told herself she'd put away her feelings for him long ago, but the moment she'd seen him, she'd known she was fooling herself. She still cared about him. The question was, how did he feel about her?

They walked into Galaxy, which featured all sorts of occult paraphernalia decorated in reassuring tones of mauve and silver.

Eugenia remembered her reaction to the shop when she'd first seen it a year ago. She'd thought Calista had cleverly allowed customers to gradually go from the familiar to something more far out. She wondered what Rafe would think about the place.

Rafe looked around the shop, taking in the decor and the subtle suggestions that there was nothing strange or threatening about Calista's wares.

"Interesting," he commented. "I'd say she knows exactly what she's doing."

"I think it makes the middle-class customers who might start with tarot and astrology feel more comfortable playing around with something more edgy," Eugenia told him. "You don't have to admit you're shopping here for anything but tarot cards. It's like Voodoo Night at my restaurant. They can say they're coming for the great food—instead of the ceremony."

"So you admit you're a good cook?"

"I know I'm a good cook."

As they were talking, a curtain at the back of the shop parted, and a petite woman with very light café au lait skin, pretty features, and short-cut, dark, curly hair stepped out. It was Calista, looking very different from the woman they'd seen last night. She was very much a modern businesswoman in her dark suit and emerald green blouse.

She stopped short when she saw Rafe. "You were there last night."

He nodded. "Eugenia hired my company to investigate the muggings."

"Uh huh. And now?"

"We'll see," he answered.

Eugenia jumped into the conversation. "Calista, I'm glad we caught you."

"I was just on my way out," the voodoo priestess answered.

Was that true, or had she made the sudden plans when she'd seen him and Eugenia?

"We'll only keep you a minute," he answered. "We'd like to ask you a few questions."

"I had enough of that from the police last night," she snapped, then seemed to make an effort to calm herself.

Rafe nodded. "So did we. But it might be good if we touched bases."

"Why?"

"Because I'd say the cops are focused on you and Eugenia, and the two of you should compare notes."

Calista thought about that, then gave a small nod.

"What about the drummer?" Eugenia asked. "Cumberland said he was illegal."

"He was subbing for my regular guy."

"Could he have done something to Villars?" Rafe asked.

"I don't think so. He didn't even know Villars. And if somebody hired him to get the man, we're out of luck because he's disappeared."

"How do you know?"

"Justin—the other drummer—told me. He's the one who recommended Lorenzo."

"Lorenzo what?

"Dill, but he could have made that up."

"Do you trust Justin?"

"Yes," she snapped, and he had the feeling he'd stumbled into a topic she didn't want to discuss. And not because it had anything to do with the case.

"Could he have tried to frame you for murder?"

"Say what?"

He held up the grocery bag he'd brought along, then turned it over and dramatically dropped the voodoo charm on the counter. It was still in its inner plastic bag wrapping—to keep outside fingerprints from contaminating the evidence.

She stared at the charm. "Where did you get that?"

"From Eugenia's doormat, after we got back from the police station last night."

"It's not from me."

"That was our assumption, but we were hoping you could tell us something about this thing."

Rafe watched Calista carefully. She was upset.

"What's your professional opinion of this?"

Calista picked up the bag by the top edge and turned it one way and then the other, looking at the lumpy object inside.

"This is bad . . ." she murmured, then raised her eyes to Eugenia. "Whoever put it on the doorstep wished you ill. But it's not skillfully made. The person didn't know a lot about the voodoo religion."

Or they were acting like they didn't, Rafe thought.

"How would they know to make it?" he asked.

She gestured toward well-stocked shelves in the back room. "There are books about making gris-gris." She laughed. "Or you could probably get directions on the Internet."

"Can I keep this?" Calista asked.

"Why?"

"I want to check out the ingredients."

"We'll need it back."

"Of course."

He cleared his throat. "I want to ask you a question."

She raised her gaze to his.

"Eugenia says you came to her with the idea of doing Voodoo Night."

"Yes."

"How did you think of the idea?"

Her gaze turned inward. "Someone suggested it to me."

"Who?"

"I do some ceremonies and demonstrations for interested groups."

"Local groups?" Rafe asked.

"They are often local. But sometimes there's a convention in town that wants to show off our unique culture. Eugenia probably told you I was giving a talk at a plantation where she was providing the food."

He nodded.

"Sometimes I speak to groups interested in New Orleans history. They usually want to hear about Marie Laveau, the famous nineteenth century Voodoo Queen. People still visit her tomb and ask for favors."

Rafe caught the note of wistfulness in Calista's voice. Probably she wished she had the woman's storied power and influence. Was that possible in today's world? And what would she do to get it?

"Back to our current situation," he said. "You said you didn't know who suggested Voodoo Night?"

"I'd done a ceremony at a hall you can rent for special occasions like weddings. And I took some questions from the audience. Someone suggested that I find an upscale place to do ceremonies on a regular basis."

Rafe kept his gaze on her. "And who was that?"

"I don't know. I had asked audience members to write down their questions on three by five cards. It was on one of the cards."

"Do you still have it?"

"No."

"Do you remember who was in the audience?"

"Some of the same people who attended the service last night. Villars. Gertie DeLong and her sister Martha Wilson."

Interesting, Rafe thought. And was she telling them everything she knew? Or was she being evasive? About what, exactly?

"Did they explicitly suggest Chez Eugenia?"

"No. I thought of the restaurant later when Eugenia and I happened to be working the same event." Calista picked up the charm, which was still in the bag, turning it in her hand. "I'll put this away for now."

"I don't think so," a man said from the doorway.

CHAPTER EIGHT

Everybody turned to see Detective Cumberland standing a few feet away looking pleased with himself.

"That thing is evidence, and it should be down at the station house in a secure location."

Rafe managed not to curse aloud. But he was pretty sure his face showed his annoyance.

Cumberland looked him up and down. "Did you have sense enough not to get your fingerprints on it?"

"Yeah. We put it into the plastic bag without touching it," Rafe answered, making an effort to keep his voice even. "And I was going to bring it in, after Calista had a look at it."

"That wasn't your decision, and asking questions is my job, not yours. So I'd appreciate it if you kept your nose out of my investigation."

Rafe couldn't stop himself from pointing out the obvious. "This thing was at Ms. Beaumont's house last night—not in the restaurant. Technically, it's not part of your case."

"We're dealing with a voodoo ceremony, and you know damn well you should have informed me."

Rafe wanted to argue that it had been pretty late when they'd found the charm. But he could see there was no use pissing off a police detective.

Cumberland focused on Rafe, and he couldn't help feeling like a suspect in a mystery novel about to be confronted with a startling revelation.

"I dug a little into your background," he said in a conversational tone. "Apparently your dad did odd jobs for the Beaumonts—when he was sober enough to know which end of a screwdriver to use."

Rafe didn't take the opportunity to protest that his father had stopped drinking years ago.

The detective's gaze flicked back and forth between Rafe and Eugenia.

"So did the two of you know each other when you were growing up? Did Gascon cart his little boy to work with him in the Beaumont mansion?" he asked.

"On occasion I came there to work with Dad," Rafe answered. "So what?"

"Cumberland shrugged. I'm examining all the angles. You did a stint in the army, then joined Decorah Security?"

"Didn't we cover that last night?"

"Not specifically. I don't like smart-assed dicks poking their noses into my cases and withholding evidence. What is Decorah Security, anyway?"

"A detective agency, like you said."

"But you specialize in weird cases."

"What of it?"

"I have to wonder if you're legit."

Rafe pulled a business card, and pointed to one of the lines. "This is our main number. You can call the owner, Frank Decorah, and talk to him if you have any questions about the agency. Or you can go to our Web site."

"I already did that," Cumberland said before turning to Eugenia. "Is the voodoo angle why you hired him? Or was it for old times' sake?"

"Neither. It was because the police department wasn't doing anything about the muggings near my restaurant."

Cumberland's eyes narrowed. Obviously he didn't like the answer. "Is that why he spent the night at your place? For protection?"

Beside him, Eugenia made a small sound. Rafe kept his gaze fixed on the detective. "Yeah, for protection. And how is our relationship relevant?"

"Everything's relevant in a murder."

"Are you saying you got the coroner's report—and Villars was murdered?"

"I don't have to share that information with you. But until we get information to the contrary, we're treating it as a murder investigation."

Before the confrontation could heat up any further, Rafe steered Eugenia out of the shop and down the sidewalk. Both of them remained silent until they'd gotten back into the car.

"Why does that guy have to be so nasty?" she asked.

"Maybe he's got some personal involvement we don't know about," he answered as he pulled away from the curb and drove slowly away. "Or maybe it's what Pete said. He's desperate to solve an important case."

Eugenia sighed. "I guess he came around to my apartment and got an earful from good old Ms. Houston."

"Yeah. I'm sorry."

"Not your fault." She turned to him. "How are you reading Calista—after this morning's discussion?"

"She's got a personal relationship with the drummer named Justin."

Her head jerked toward him. "How do you know?"

"I don't know for sure, but my asking about him made her edgy."

"What if they cooked up a murder together?"

"I suppose it's possible, but she'd be playing a dangerous game. What would be her motivation for going after Villars? She's trying to build her career, and she doesn't need to be tainted by suspicion of murder."

Eugenia shook her head. "In some circles it would be a potent demonstration of her powers."

"In front of a lot of witnesses," Rafe pointed out.

"Do you have other people you want to question?"

"Yes. Everybody there. But I want to check something first." He was already a few blocks from Calista's shop. He started looking for a parking place. When he found one, he pulled to the curb.

"What are you doing?"

"Taking precautions."

He climbed out and walked around the vehicle, checking under the bumpers and along the sides. When his fingers encountered something that shouldn't be there, he cursed under his breath and got back into the car.

Eugenia studied his expression. "What is it?"

"Somebody put a tracking device on the car."

"What do you mean?"

"Someone wants to know where we're going."

"Who?"

"Cumberland would be a good bet."

"Is that legal?"

"No, but I don't think that would stop him. You might wonder how he showed up at Calista's shop right after we did."

"Did you take it off?" she asked anxiously.

"No."

"Why not?"

"Because I've got a better idea."

He drove back to the parking space in back of the restaurant. Then he got out of the car, found the device again and removed it—placing it at the entrance to the patio.

"It's going to look like we came back here and stayed," he said.

"That's clever."

He answered with a shrug.

"What are we doing instead?" she asked as he climbed back into the car.

He wanted to tell her she should go inside and relax, but he wasn't entirely comfortable with that. Not when someone had been sneaking around in the alley the night before.

"You had a patron die a few months ago, didn't you?"

"Uh, yes. I feel like you have a whole case file on me."

"Actually, I do."

She sucked in a breath. "I don't much like that."

"If I'm going to take a job, I want as much background as

possible. The woman who died was named Wilma Saxon. What can you tell me about her?"

"She was a friend of Gertie DeLong and Martha Wilson."

"Who started coming to the meetings first?"

"I think they showed up around the same time, but I wasn't exactly keeping a scorecard."

"Did she and Villars know each other?"

"I think so, but I wasn't poking into the backgrounds of my customers. There wasn't any reason to do it."

He looked toward the crime-scene tape blocking the restaurant's kitchen door. "That was true—before the crawfish etouffee hit the fan yesterday. Now we want to know as much as possible. Did they pay with credit cards?"

"Some did. Some didn't."

"And you didn't take the roll each time."

"That's right." She leaned back against the headrest, closed her eyes and thought back over previous Voodoo Nights. "I think the Villars might have been there once or twice before."

"Okay."

She sat up straighter and looked at him, then away.

"You had kind of a rough morning," he murmured.

"So did you."

"I'm used to being hassled by the local police departments."

"Why?"

"It's not just Cumberland. Some cops resent private detectives dabbling in their cases."

"You're not dabbling."

"If not, from his point of view, then I'm interfering." When she started to speak, he rushed ahead. "You don't have to keep defending me. I'm putting it in his terms."

She kept her eyes on him, and he couldn't pull his own gaze away from her.

Eight years ago, she'd hurt him badly, and it had taken a long time to get over it. Maybe he never had, since he hadn't married. But seeing her again had brought back more of the good feelings than the bad ones. For a long time after she'd broken off with him, he'd told himself that rich Miss Beaumont had only been playing with the son of the handyman. And as soon as he'd gone away, she'd forgotten all about him.

He'd resented her for that. But the resentment had evaporated long ago. Looking back, he'd been enchanted with her, but he hadn't understood her. Or maybe back then she'd been waiting to find out who she really was. Now he could see what she'd become. She wasn't trading on her family name to get ahead in the restaurant business. And she was working damn hard to make it. She'd even thought of a creative way to bring more people to her restaurant—although that hadn't worked out so well.

Coming back to New Orleans and seeing her had generated powerful emotions. He wanted very badly to kiss her again. Which he knew was a stupid move. But just to prove he could do it without going up in smoke, he bent and brushed his lips to hers.

It was like tossing a match into dry tinder. Heat flared, burning through his resolve.

Or perhaps it was her response that caught and held him. She didn't resist or pull away. She leaned in, making it clear that she'd been thinking there was unfinished business between them.

Was she trying to test her own reaction to him? He didn't want to examine her motives. He just wanted to be with her in the moment.

He gathered her to him, deepening the kiss, angling his head to drink in everything he could from this woman he had wanted for what seemed like centuries.

She moved closer, her arms creeping around his neck as she kissed him with the same intensity. He'd told himself the car was a safe place to kiss her. Not like her apartment where they had too much privacy. Now he couldn't stop an image of pulling her into his lap so that he could make love with her.

He fought a war with himself, then finally lifted his head, staring into her eyes as they both struggled to drag in full breaths.

"Come inside."

His body and his emotions urged him to say yes. Instead he managed to say, "No."

CHAPTER NINE

Calista wanted to turn the "Open" sign at her front door to "Closed," but she resisted the urge. Better not to do anything out of pattern. Or let the cops see how shaken she was by what had happened last night at the ceremony.

And she hated being a murder suspect. Too bad she wasn't white and powerful—with the clout to get that damn police detective off her back—or Rafe Gascon, for that matter. He was much too perceptive.

It flitted through her mind to make a couple of voodoo dolls with their names on them and poke pins in their vital organs. It might work or it might not. But probably murdering the lead detective on the case and the man Eugenia had hired to protect her wasn't the way to go. Could she find something on either one of them? Something she could use?

She went into the back room and sat down in the big overstuffed chair where she could relax when there were no customers out front. With her eyes closed, she thought about the two men. She'd bet Cumberland had something he wanted to keep hidden. Most people did. But Gascon was another matter. He gave her the impression that he didn't give a damn who knew what about him. She turned that last thought over in her mind for a few moments, then decided it didn't quite fit. There *was* something about him that he'd prefer not to discuss in public. Could she find out what it was and twist it to her advantage?

When nothing came to her immediately, she turned her attention in another direction, thinking about how she'd gotten here from her own humble beginnings in the bayou country. Out near Houma.

For starters, her name had been Sandra back then. Her daddy had left her momma before his daughter had much memory of him. Sandra had been on track to spend her life working as a maid for rich white folks like her momma did when a lucky incident had changed her life. Denada, a voodoo priestess had gotten into some trouble in New Orleans and had come back to her old neighborhood to take herself out of the public eye for a while.

In fact, she'd taken off after the death of a white lover who'd spent the night with her and died of a heart attack. She'd come back to her family home like New Orleans royalty, and Calista had met her at the country store where the kids bought soda pop and candy bars and hung out in the afternoons.

She'd been fascinated by Denada's long colorful gowns, her cultured accent and the headdress that added six inches to her height. And the teenaged Sandra tagged along when the priestess went out into the swamp to gather herbs and roots to use in potions and ceremonies.

Denada had rather liked having an apprentice hanging on her every word. She'd helped Calista pick a sexier name, and she'd started teaching her which herbs were used for what. And she'd also taught her voodoo rituals. In her lessons, she'd made it clear that attitude was as important as substance. If you had a commanding presence, people listened to you.

When Denada had said she was going back to the Big Easy, Calista had begged to go along. Her mother had warned against the dangers of the city, but Calista hadn't wanted to listen. How could the city be worse than the poverty of her hardscrabble existence? She'd gone to New Orleans with her mentor and found out that a girl from the bayou country had a lot of catching up to do. But she'd listened and learned and never looked back. She hadn't graduated from high school, but she'd picked up more from the priestess than she could in any school.

The year she'd turned sixteen, Denada had introduced her to a man who had more to teach her. About the sexual pleasure in giving and receiving pain. And about how to use sex to wield power over others. That had gotten her into trouble a time or two. But it had also become very important to her.

She liked the life she'd created for herself. And she might not admit it to Rafe Gascon or anyone else, but she did have ambitions of becoming the Marie Laveau of this generation. The woman had been a force in New Orleans at a time when women had been chattel. And with Denada married and living in the islands, she had a shot at it.

Marie Laveau had overthrown the other voodoo queens in the city and built a power base. She'd made predictions about the future, performed exorcisms, and offered sacrifices to the voodoo gods in private rituals behind her cottage on St. Ann Street.

Of course, she'd also been a devout Catholic, which didn't quite work for Calista. She had long ago decided the teachings of the church were just a way of keeping the common folks in line.

She let her mind wander, thinking of those glory days of voodoo and of how New Orleans had changed since Laveau's times. With modern communications and transportation, the city was more tuned to the culture beyond its borders. It was also more sophisticated in many ways. But there were strong ties to the past, and a strong woman might grab the old-time power for herself. Power meant security.

Or was she just dreaming about how to get herself out of the mess that had swirled up around her in the middle of that ceremony last night?

Calista's cell phone rang, and she looked at the caller ID, then pressed the answer button.

"You said you would meet me," Jillian Hargrave said.

"I got hung up here. Eugenia and that Rafe Gascon guy came over with some gris-gris someone had left on her doorstep."

The woman on the end of the phone line caught her breath. "Did you make it?"

"No."

"Then who?"

"I have no idea."

"Are we in danger" Jillian asked.

"No. But I don't like the way Cumberland showed up right after Eugenia and Gascon. I think it's better if we don't meet. We don't want anyone seeing us together and wondering why."

"I'm frightened."

"Hang tight."

"I'm trying."

When Eugenia turned toward the door, Rafe put a hand on her arm.

"Sorry. I've got to keep my mind where it belongs."

"Which is where?" she asked in a barely audible voice.

"You hired Decorah Security to do a job—and they sent me to do it. And it's turned into something neither one of us expected."

He was talking about the case, but he could just as well have been talking about the two of them—about the feelings that had sprung back to life when they'd laid eyes on each other.

She flopped back into her seat. "Was it a coincidence that they sent you?"

He thought about the answer. "I've come to believe that nothing Frank Decorah does is a coincidence."

"You mentioned him to Cumberland."

"Yeah. There's something about Frank that sets him apart."

"What do you mean?"

"It's hard to explain, but once you start working for him, you know you don't want to be the agent who screws up an assignment." He kept his gaze on her. "But it's not just about Frank. You won't be safe until we figure out what's going on. Not just the muggings. We need to understand what happened to Villars—and why that voodoo charm showed up on your doorstep."

She dragged in a breath and let it out. "You're right."

Some of the tension eased out of him. "I don't like leaving you, but it should be okay during the day."

"Where are you going?"

"To do some more poking around."

"And you're not going to share your plans with me?"

"Routine stuff that has to be taken care of." He gave her his cell number. "If anything unusual happens, call me immediately."

She promised to do that, and they separated.

Although Rafe could have worked on his computer at Eugenia's house, he figured it was better to put some distance between them.

He'd said he was going to work, but he decided that a couple hours sleep wouldn't be a bad idea.

The sleep helped clear his brain, and when he touched

the back of his head, the lump he'd gotten the night before was almost gone.

Feeling better, he put on his dark robe and practiced some martial arts moves in the hotel room to get his circulation going. Then he straightened the covers, plumped up the pillows, and grabbed his laptop. First he wrote out a report for Frank Decorah of what had happened so far. Then he switched to research. But Eugenia kept invading his thoughts.

Ordering himself to stick to business, he plowed through a bunch of background investigations, including on the man Pete had told him about, Sam Gunderson, the rival who'd fought Villars to buy a boutique hotel. There was an online article showing pictures of the hotel and talking about its excellent reputation. Apparently Villars' slander hadn't done the place any harm.

Rafe went back to trying to draw connections between the people who had been at the voodoo ceremony.

He started by focusing on Wilma Saxon, the woman who had come to some of the ceremonies and then died.

She'd been ninety-two and had apparently died of a stroke. Too bad they still didn't have the cause of death for Villars.

Wilma had been married to a man who had left her well off when he'd died twenty-five years earlier, and she'd belonged to the same social circle as Gertie DeLong and Martha Wilson. They'd played bridge together on a regular basis.

And she'd dabbled in an investment club that was run by —wait for it—Martin Villars.

An interesting piece of information, Rafe decided as he dug up background on the club. There were a number of investors, including Gertie and Martha.

What had Villars done with the money they'd given him to invest? Rafe followed that trail and discovered that he'd lost at least forty thousand dollars for each of them.

Was that a motive for murder? Maybe not with women who still had sizable fortunes, but he kept the information on his radar.

He'd been trying to stay away from Eugenia, but he decided he had a legitimate reason to phone her.

"Hi," she said in a tentative voice that told him she'd looked at her caller ID.

"Hi." He cleared his throat. "I'm going to interview Gertie or Martha. Which would you start with?"

"What's your interest in them?"

"Apparently they were in an investment club with Villars, along with Wilma Saxon."

"I had no idea."

"Well, he lost a lot of money for all of them."

"You're sure about that?"

"Yes. Which sister seems to be the driving force in the relationship?"

"I guess Gertie."

"So I can start with her."

"We."

He could have protested. Instead he said, "If you're not busy, we can do it now."

"Okay."

After pulling into the alley, he called her on his cell again, annoyed with himself that he was nervous about seeing her—as opposed to fantasizing about her.

When she came down, it was obvious that she was on edge with him, too, and he wanted to ask why she'd insisted on getting back together.

Instead of focusing on the two of them, he went right to the case. "If Villars was murdered, it could be by anyone in the restaurant. Even one of the tourists."

"Why would a tourist murder him?"

"Why would anyone? I mean, all kinds of weird stuff happens. Like that woman who pushed a man she didn't know under a subway train."

"I guess that's right."

"Or one of the tourists could have been a hit man."

She snorted. "Like that ditz-brain woman who wanted to know if zombies were part of the service?"

"Well, maybe not her, although someone posing as a tourist could have had a beef with him. But back to the locals, what do you know about Gertie and Martha?"

"Not a lot. They're both nice old ladies."

"From good families. They're both widows. Gertie's husband died thirty years ago. Martha was widowed only about five years ago."

"I didn't know any of that."

He switched back to the dead man. "From your point of view, what kind of guy was Villars?"

"He could be very charming. Or he could be annoying and impatient. It depended on which week," she answered.

"Why do you think that was true?"

"He could have been bipolar. Or he could have been the kind of person who takes out his moods on other people."

"Did he like spending money, or was he conservative?"

"Conservative. He liked ordering the daily special."

"How was his relationship with his wife?"

"They seemed okay. But they could have been the kind of couple who put on a good face in public."

He nodded. "Yeah. Feel free to share if you think of anything else pertinent about him." He pulled out his cell phone again and found the address he'd copied down the night before. "Have you ever been to Gertie's house?"

"No."

"It's in the Garden District." He drove up St. Charles, away from the French Quarter to the part of town that had been settled by the English. In the French Quarter, the houses were cheek to jowl, sometimes with courtyards between them like at Eugenia's restaurant. In the Garden District, the property around each house was more extensive, with elaborately tended green space.

"Only a few blocks from your old house," he said as he turned onto Halaconia Street."

"Right. I didn't know. Shouldn't we call ahead to let her know we're coming?"

"Actually, no. it's better to take her by surprise."

"Why?"

"So she doesn't have time to make up a story."

"You think she would?"

"It depends on if she's got something to hide." He looked toward Eugenia momentarily. "I think our best approach is to put the emphasis on Villars, not her."

They parked in the driveway of Gertie's rambling Victorian house. The driveway led back to a detached garage much like the garage where Rafe and Eugenia had spent so many happy hours, and he felt his stomach clench. Was she thinking about *that?* he wondered as he cut her a quick glance. Maybe, because she turned quickly up the walk that led to the house.

It was one of the New Orleans painted ladies where the siding was one color and the trim was done up in several complementing or contrasting shades. In this case, the siding was a light mauve, and the trim was in deeper mauve, brown and green, although the paint job was beginning to fade a bit.

When they rang the bell, it took almost a minute for them to hear any sign of movement inside.

"Just a minute," a voice called.

Finally a wrinkled hand pulled a lace curtain away from the glass at the sidelight. When she saw who it was, Gertie opened the door. Her hair was dyed much too dark, giving her face a pasty appearance.

"Why Eugenia, dear, what are you doing here?"

"We were hoping to get some information about Martin Villars," Rafe said.

"Oh, that poor man."

"Can we come in?"

The old woman's hands fluttered. "Where are my manners? Come out to the garden room. Would you like a glass of iced tea?"

Rafe was about to decline when Eugenia said, "We'd love some."

He realized that was probably a smart move. Letting Ms.

DeLong serve them refreshments would relax her and make the interview go more smoothly.

They walked to the back of the house, through a kitchen that looked like it had been renovated in the nineties, and from there to a room that spanned the back of the house. It had apparently been converted from a back porch, the screens replaced by a bank of windows that looked out over a huge yard. Wicker chairs and tables were arranged to take advantage of the garden view—which was a bit wilder than Rafe might have expected. Apparently Gertie wasn't having the garden service as often as she really needed.

"Just have a seat, and I'll be right back," Gertie murmured as she bustled away.

Rafe crossed to the nearest window and looked out at the yard, then settled into one of the wicker chairs next to Eugenia.

From digging into her finances, he knew that Gertie was well off, but either she was trying to save money, or she simply didn't believe in pouring a lot of cash into her property.

She returned in a few minutes carrying a tray with a pitcher of iced tea, glasses and a plate of cookies.

"Let me," he said, springing up to take the tray from her and set it on the coffee table.

Their hostess gestured toward the tea and cookies. "Please take some."

Rafe did. They were a well-known upscale brand, giving a hint at Gertie's spending priorities.

She pulled one of the chairs around to face them.

"Do the police know yet what happened to poor Martin?"

"We haven't heard anything," Eugenia said after taking a sip of tea. "This is good."

"Praise from the famous Eugenia Beaumont is praise indeed."

"I'm not famous," Eugenia protested.

"You will be. And not for the wrong reasons. Your food is outstanding. And a nice mix of the innovative and the classic."

"I didn't know you were a discerning food critic," Rafe said.

The older woman flushed. "My late husband was very choosy about restaurant meals. He gave me an appreciation for top-notch cuisine."

"Thank you," Eugenia said.

"Did you happen to see what Mr. Villars was doing before he went down?" Rafe asked.

She looked abashed. "Sorry. I was watching the voodoo priestess."

"I think most of us were," Eugenia agreed.

"Then all hell broke loose, as they say," the older woman murmured

Eugenia nodded.

"How long have you been going to Voodoo Night?" Rafe asked.

"Off and on since it started," the older woman said.

"How did you hear about it?" he asked.

"I had gone to a meeting where Calista was giving a demonstration. Then I got a postcard telling me that she was going to be having regular ceremonies at Eugenia's restaurant."

Rafe nodded. "Was Martin Villars at that other demonstration?"

"I don't think so. There was a large audience." She thought for a moment, "but I think Holly, his wife, was there."

"Why are so many upper- and middle-class white people interested in voodoo, do you think?" Rafe asked.

"I can't answer for everyone else, but I find it fascinating. It's so different from our Western tradition. More tied to nature. You know it was brought over by African slaves?"

"Yes."

"And the New Orleans version is different from the Haitian."

"How?" Rafe asked.

"The slaves who were brought here were more likely to be kept in family groups than was the custom farther east. That cemented a stronger African community, which meant their culture and spirituality stayed vibrant."

Rafe nodded.

"And of course gris-gris was more important in the New Orleans version of the religions than the Haitian. It started with amulets for protection—and to poison enemies."

"Poison. Interesting."

"And this is where the voodoo doll tradition comes from."

"You know a lot about it," Rafe said.

"If I'm interested in a subject, I do research."

"On the Web?"

She smiled. "I do use the Web, but I prefer the old-fashioned way—books."

"Did you get some from Calista Lacoste's shop?"

"Why, yes. She had an excellent selection."

"Did you ever try to make a voodoo charm?"

"Gertie laughed. "I wouldn't go *quite* that far."

Rafe leaned toward her. "I also wanted to ask you about Villars' investment club."

She looked startled. "How do you know about that?"

"I was checking into his background. He lost a lot of members' money when the stock market went down."

Her face hardened. "At the time, I was angry about that. Then I decided that he didn't control the market, and it wasn't exactly his fault. On the other hand, I never trusted him again with financial matters."

"That sounds wise," Eugenia said.

"Would anybody in the club have been angry enough to take revenge?" Rafe asked.

"Oh my, I don't think so," Gertie answered, but it was hard to be sure if she was telling the truth or only wishing it was true.

They talked for a few more minutes, before Rafe asked, "Is there anything else you want to tell us?"

Gertie thought for a moment, "Did the priestess get her knife back?"

Rafe's head swung to her. "What do you mean?"

"I saw it on the floor. Then I think someone kicked it under the radiator in the scuffle."

"I don't know," Rafe said. "But we'll certainly check. Thanks for the tip."

He wanted to rush back to the restaurant immediately, but he wasn't simply going to get up and dash out. Finally he said, "Thanks for your help."

When they got up, he forced himself to keep his pace slow. But apparently he hadn't fooled Eugenia about his intentions. As soon as they were outside, she said, "You want that knife."

"Yeah."

"Why is it important?" she asked as they climbed into the car. "It wasn't used against Villars."

"Before the ceremony started, I picked it up—and got one of my visions."

"I saw that. But you didn't say much about it—besides that it had happened."

"At the time, I thought it might be a distraction that I didn't need. Now I think it could be important."

"And you want to go back to the vision and see what you can discover now?"

"Yes."

"All right. But isn't the restaurant a crime scene?"

"Yeah, but you'll go in the back way and see if the knife is where Gertie said it went."

"What about you?"

"I'm going to watch out for the cops—and your nosy neighbor." He stopped and started again. "Unless you don't want to risk going in there."

"I'll do it. To get the knife and to see what kind of mess is in there."

They returned to the restaurant, and Rafe pulled up in the parking space out back.

"If you find it, wrap it in a napkin and bring it out."

"Okay," Eugenia answered, glancing back at Rafe, who climbed out of the car and leaned against the fender, watching the alley. Now that she was here and saw the crime-scene tape again, she didn't much like breaking the law, but she knew Rafe was right. The knife could be a clue. It was also evidence that Cumberland would want, the same way he'd wanted the gris-gris. But they knew that Villars hadn't been stabbed, so the knife could only be marginally useful to the cops. On the other hand, it could give Rafe a lot of information. She hoped.

She looked back at him, then unlocked the kitchen door and ducked under the tape so she could step inside. When she closed the door, the room was dark inside, but she knew she couldn't turn on the lights. Instead she waited for her eyes to adjust, then winced when she took in the scene.

The room was the way she had left it. She and her sous-chef, David, had partially cleaned up after the dinner, but she hadn't gotten a chance to finish the job because she'd been busy with her guests. And David and her dishwasher had been herded out with everyone else.

She was always prompt with clean up. Now she stood for a moment with her hands on her hips, staring at the mess of day-old, dirty pots and pans, plus some dishes that had come back from the dining room. Stifling the urge to start putting things into the sink, she tiptoed through the kitchen, conscious of the way her footsteps echoed on the tile floor. Her breath caught when she saw the real mess, which was in the dining room. Nobody had touched the place except the crime-scene techs, who had left a disaster. Some tables and chairs were overturned, scattering food and pieces of broken plates onto the floor. Other plates of day-old food still sat on tables.

And Calista's equipment was still in the restaurant, including the drums that the men had been using and the women's tambourines. She'd have to arrange to get those back to her when it was all right to come in here.

Eugenia wrinkled her nose as she wove her way through the wreckage. The knife had started on the table with the other voodoo paraphernalia, like the candles and the skull. But Calista had picked it up. And Gertie said it had gone under the radiator.

Eugenia got down on her hands and knees, reached under the radiator, and felt nothing. Was Gertie wrong?

She crawled along on all fours, still searching blindly for the knife. When a piece of broken plate nicked her hand, she made a strangled sound, then involuntarily looked up to make sure nobody had heard her.

Pulling out her hand, she looked at the small drop of blood she'd drawn and wiped it away on the leg of her jeans.

Moving more cautiously, she kept looking for the knife. Just when she was about to give up, she finally found it wedged against the baseboard. After pulling it out, she held it up to the light, examining the ornate handle. It was the knife she remembered from the night before.

After wrapping it in the napkin, she started for the back door.

She stopped in her tracks when she heard Rafe talking to someone. Of all the people it could have been, it turned out to be detective Cumberland.

"What are you doing here?" the detective said.

"Eugenia's apartment is upstairs. That's not a crime scene, is it?" Rafe said, pitching his voice loud enough to make sure she would hear it from inside.

"No. But it would be a crime to go inside the restaurant. She could tamper with evidence in there. Where is she?"

She heard Rafe's calm answer. Deceptively calm. "She went around the corner to get something."

"What?"

"She didn't say."

"I'm going inside the restaurant," the detective said.

CHAPTER TEN

Rafe was screaming inside his mind, warning Eugenia to get the hell out of there, as he watched Cumberland use a key to unlock the door. But where could she go? Not out the front door, because then her nosy neighbor, Mrs. Houston, would likely see her—and report that she'd ignored the crime-scene tape.

Cumberland stepped into the kitchen and Rafe followed. The detective didn't stop him, perhaps because he was sure Eugenia was in here, and he wanted to confront the two of them together.

He took a quick look around the kitchen, then crossed to a large cupboard and pulled the door open. Eugenia wasn't inside.

Cumberland opened a few more cupboards before proceeding into the dining room. Rafe winced when he saw it, imagining Eugenia's reaction.

The detective strode to the front of the room and whipped aside the curtains, but Eugenia wasn't behind them. He turned in a circle, searching for hiding places, obviously puzzled that he hadn't found what he was looking for.

Rafe followed his gaze, wondering where she'd gone. Hopefully not out the front. More likely she was still in here, if she'd figured out where to hide.

Cumberland strode confidently around the room, looking under tables and even getting down on his knees to inspect the radiator.

He snarled and pulled his hand back.

"What?"

"I cut myself on a piece of broken glass."

"Gee, that's too bad."

"I don't need any comments from you," he said, snatching up a napkin and wrapping it around his hand.

Rafe didn't point out that this fishing expedition had been Cumberland's idea, and now he was disturbing the scene.

Rafe started to relax a little as he watched the detective run out of places to look. Finally he said something under his breath that Rafe couldn't catch, strode back to the kitchen, and went through more cupboards. When he struck out again, he gave Rafe a dark look and returned to the parking area, where he was apparently having trouble not kicking the wall in frustration.

"Maybe I'll wait until Ms. Beaumont comes back."

"Did you have something specific to say to her? Like did the autopsy report come back?"

"No," the detective snapped.

No it hadn't come back? Or no he wasn't going to share

the information with her? Rafe decided it was better not to ask.

They both waited for several minutes, neither of them speaking as Rafe ordered himself not to let his tension get the better of him. Finally Cumberland silently strode through the patio to the unmarked car he'd left out at the curb.

Rafe stayed where he was, watching for Mrs. Houston or Cumberland to pop back around the corner and catch him conferring with Eugenia at the back door.

A few moments later, the door did open a sliver, and Eugenia peeked out. "All clear?"

"Yeah."

She stepped into the alley, then closed the door behind her. Without waiting for him to follow, she crossed quickly to the courtyard and unlocked the door to her apartment. Not until she was upstairs did she face him and breathe out a sigh.

"I heard him searching the place."

"I kept expecting him to whoop for joy. Where were you?"

"You know the wainscoting in the front room?"

"Yeah."

"It's built so there's a panel that I can open. I keep some supplies behind it."

"I'm glad the bastard didn't find you. He really thought he was going to catch us at something illegal."

She laughed. "Sorry to disappoint him."

"You have the knife?"

"Yes." She pulled the napkin from the waistband of her slacks and unwrapped it.

"Thanks. I'm sorry I put you through that."

"It worked out. What do you think you're going to find out?"

"I'm not sure. But I want to be sitting down when I touch it."

"Okay." She set the knife on the coffee table.

Rafe sat down on the sofa and looked at the ornate handle of the weapon. Last time the experience with it had taken him by surprise. This time he had a better idea of what to expect, and he hoped he could exercise more control.

Might as well get it over with. He reached out and pressed his fingers to the handle of the knife, thinking that he could pull away if he needed to. But he was wrong.

An invisible force grabbed him, melding his flesh to the cold metal.

He heard Eugenia gasp and wondered what she saw. But that was the last conscious thought of the man sitting in her living room.

He was someone else. He wasn't sure who, but he was standing in the bayou clearing that he'd seen before. Last time he'd come back to himself pretty quickly because he'd thought he was only caught in a side trip. This time the vision had sucked him in, and he had more time to take in his surroundings. Even though he was in someone else's body, he did have some control of his observations. He heard the call of birds and the splash of something slithering into the water. He saw a great egret flap away as he approached.

He was in another person's body, but he hung on to

enough of Rafe Gascon's consciousness to be aware of what he was supposed to be doing.

He looked around at the thick vegetation surrounded him on three sides. Towering above him were cypress and tupelo trees, dripping with Spanish moss. Closer to the ground were dwarf palmettos and flowers he couldn't name. Thirty yards away he could see brown water moving sluggishly between low banks where cypress roots held the soil in place. A pier jutted out into the water, and he saw a boat tied up. Not a traditional Cajun pirogue, but what looked like a very modern speedboat. The name on the side was. . . .

Had he stepped into a scene in the not-too-distant past? Or was this something that had taken place months or years ago?

He looked down at his legs. He was wearing jeans and heavy boots suitable for tramping around in the backcountry.

When he held up a hand, he saw that he was wearing leather gloves.

He opened his mind to the person whose body he shared and felt a jolt of shock. They were thinking about a slave rebellion more than two hundred years ago, when a group of brave and desperate black men rose up against their cruel masters. Three ringleaders gathered a force of five hundred slaves who stole military uniforms and weapons from a federal arsenal and marched on New Orleans. When they ran out of ammunition, they were slaughtered by a force of planters supported by the U.S. Military.

Although they were ultimately defeated, it was the best-organized slave rebellion in the history of the country.

The gory details of what the slaves had done and what

had been done to them sickened Rafe, yet the person thinking about the uprising admired the courage of the rebels. You had to be bold enough to seize the moment and change your destiny—even if you were taking a terrible risk.

Rafe didn't understand the context, but he felt the determination of the person in the bayou as they strode toward a small building that might have been a wooden toolshed.

They threw open double doors, and he goggled at what he saw inside.

There was a raised platform made from two wide boards resting on bricks. The board was covered with a wooden tray. Various objects were placed on the shelf. There were a couple of small candles, a naked voodoo doll with a pin sticking in its chest and a bundle of straw next to it. At the side was a photograph, probably of a man, although someone had scratched back and forth across the face so that the features were unrecognizable.

He saw it all through a red haze. Was that real, or was it generated by the anger of the person who had set up this altar?

When he felt a hand on his shoulder, he whirled, not sure what he was going to face.

CHAPTER ELEVEN

It was Eugenia that he saw. Her touch had pulled him back into her living room, his ears ringing and his vision still tinged with red.

"Are you all right?" she asked urgently.

He took a quick inventory. "I think so. Why did you yank me out of there?"

"You looked horrible. I mean kind of sick."

"There was a lot of yucky stuff."

"Do you want some water?"

"Yeah, that would be good."

She went to the refrigerator, got out a bottle of cold water and brought it back to him, sitting in an easy chair opposite him so that they could see each other.

"Can you tell me about it?"

He nodded, wishing he didn't have to share the information with her. But he had no right to hold it back. "Have you heard of a slave rebellion in New Orleans in the early eighteen hundreds?"

"No."

"I think it was hushed up at the time, but there was a book written about it not too long ago.

"How do you know?"

"The person . . . I shared consciousness with was thinking about it. A group of slaves who lived on a plantation with a particularly cruel master killed his son and tried to kill him, but he got away and went for help. The slaves got a bunch of others to join them in them in a rebellion. They got weapons and uniforms from a federal arsenal and marched on New Orleans. They thought they could take over the city, but a force of desperate plantation owners plus the U.S. Army caught up with them in a cane field."

When he stopped speaking, Eugenia asked, "What happened?"

"Well, obviously the slaves didn't win. They killed some of the plantation owners, but in the end they ran out of ammunition, and some awful stuff was done to them. Like putting their heads on pikes and hanging up their dismembered bodies. And that's just a rough idea of the brutality."

She gagged. "What does that have to do with a knife that was going to be used at a voodoo ceremony?"

"I'm not exactly sure. I went into the mind of a person out in the bayou. They were thinking about the rebellion as they went to the voodoo shrine they'd set up. They were thinking that the slaves were heroes for what they'd tried to do."

"Who was it? I mean, the person in the bayou."

"I don't know."

"That's all you got. Someone thinking about a slave rebellion?"

"They were comparing themselves to the slaves, thinking that they were going up against a superior force. Only they were going to be the winner. And they weren't going to use a gun. They were going to use voodoo."

She looked at the knife. "Calista was going to use that in the ceremony? Was it her?"

"I don't think so."

"Why not?"

"Because in that vision, she would have been smoother and more practiced about the voodoo part."

"So someone might have wanted her to have that particular knife—for a reason we don't know about.'"

"Maybe it's symbolic, like the slave rebellion."

"Back to—why do you think the shrine wasn't Calista's?"

"It looked like it belonged to someone starting out. They'd built an altar out in a bayou clearing, in an old shed. It had a raised platform inside." He described the contents as best he could.

"The doll and the picture must have been of someone they hated."

"Could you tell who it was?"

"In the picture, his face had been scratched out, but I'm guessing it was Villars—since he was the one who ended up dead."

"Because this person killed him?"

"Yeah. I'd like to see the autopsy report. Did they hex him to death?"

"You think that's possible?"

"If the victim believes it's possible."

"But the photo in the shrine could have just as well been Cumberland, because he's conducting the investigation."

"I don't think so. Villars was only killed yesterday. And I don't see the future. Only the past." He thought about the angle of the sun. "I'm guessing it was days ago, in the morning. Maybe the person was getting ready for the ceremony at the restaurant. Maybe asking for the blessing of the gods."

She shuddered. "Do you think you could find the altar?"

He considered the question. "I wish I could. It was in a bayou clearing, and there were no landmarks that I recognized." He stopped, thinking there was something that might have been a clue. But he couldn't recall it now.

Eugenia interrupted his thoughts.

"And what do you make of the whole scene?"

"Someone is out for revenge. Like those slaves."

"I guess."

"You don't agree?"

"I don't know." She thought for a moment. "You say you were in someone's body. Couldn't you see yourself?"

"I saw legs covered in jeans and shoes with hiking boots. And hands covered with leather gloves."

"Was it a man or a woman?"

"I don't know."

He leaned his head back and closed his eyes, sitting there for a few moments until the cushion shifted. He opened his eyes and saw Eugenia leaning over him.

"That was hard on you. And that blow on the head the other night didn't help. I think you've done all you can for the moment."

"Maybe not. There's something I should be remembering."

"Sometimes the best way to remember is not to focus on the thing."

He could have asked, "And do what?"

But he didn't have to when she brought her lips to his, pressing and then withdrawing in silent invitation. He had ached to get back to where they'd been in the car, but he'd set his own feelings aside. Now she was telling him to stop backing away from her.

He shouldn't succumb. She was a client. But there was a lot of history between them, urging both of them not to deny their feelings.

He'd gone away thinking that she'd broken off with him. She'd told him it wasn't true, which still left the question of what had happened. But he couldn't focus on that now.

She moved her lips against his, nibbling, brushing back and forth, urging a response from him—and he gave it gladly.

His hand stroked up and down her ribs, inching toward the sides of her breasts, waiting for her to stop him, but she didn't.

Her body was familiar to him. Back when they'd been teenagers, they'd done everything together except have intercourse. She'd set the rules, and he'd followed them. Because he would take anything he could have with her. Now he knew fooling around wouldn't satisfy him. And he hoped she felt the same way.

Their eyes locked as she knitted her fingers with his and led him to the bed they'd shared for a few hours the night before—when he hadn't been in any kind of shape for messing around.

There was no hesitation or uncertainty about what they were going to do. After taking his gun from the waistband of his pants, he set it on the dresser. Turning, he wrapped his arms around her, and they exchanged hot kisses, swaying together as they stroked each other.

"I don't think I can stand up much longer," she whispered.

"Yeah."

He brought her down to the mattress, struggling to catch his breath. He was ready to make love with her. More than ready, but he knew he had to slow down. With his eyes closed, he worked his hands under her shirt, running his fingers over the silky skin of her back. She was so familiar to him. Dear to him. That realization sent a shock wave through him.

"What?"

"I'm having trouble believing this is real."

"It is, chérie," he said.

They held each other for long moments, until she said, "Help me get undressed."

Glad to oblige, he unhooked her bra, and she pulled it off, along with her shirt.

With a deep sigh, he buried his face between her breasts, feeling like he had finally come home after a long, lonely trip. She clasped him to her, stroking her fingers through his hair. He turned his head, swirling his tongue around one hardened nipple. When he sucked it into his mouth, she gasped his name.

"I've longed for you to do that again."

He'd longed for it, too, but he hadn't been able to admit it, even to himself.

He had a problem now. He didn't want to break the contact with her, but that was the only to get undressed. He kissed her breast, then sat up and pulled his shirt over his head.

Coming back to her, he clasped her to him, sighing at the skin-to-skin contact.

She was warm and pliant in his arms, and he swayed her breasts against his chest, making them both murmur in pleasure. Yet he had to ask, "Are you sure about this?"

"Very sure. I want everything we can give each other."

She lay back on the bed, smiling up at him as she unbuttoned and unzipped her jeans, doing a kind of striptease lying down. Lifting her hips, she pulled the jeans down and kicked them away. When she wore only her bikini panties, she slipped a finger under the top edge and ran it around the elastic.

He heard himself make a strangled sound as he watched her. Unable to help himself, he reached under the elastic, slowly easing down the panties, uncovering the triangle of blond hair at the top of her legs.

"Lord, I'm glad you didn't shave down there."

"Why?"

"It's not the way I pictured you." Had he given too much away with that comment? She only nodded, then raised her hips again so that she could slip off the panties.

When she was naked, she reached for the button at the top of his jeans, opening it and lowering his zipper.

Her gaze never left him as she slipped her hand inside, below his briefs, closing her fingers around his cock. Her familiar touch threatened to send him up in flames.

"Better not do too much of that," he gasped.

He got rid of his jeans and briefs, kicking them off onto the floor before pulling her back into his embrace, his breath catching at the way her naked body fit against his.

He held her in his arms, sliding his lips against her cheek, before coming back to her mouth for a kiss that made his head spin. He had dreamed of this. So many times. Eugenia naked with him on a real bed.

He teased her nipples with one hand, tugging and twisting them, while the other hand drifted slowly down her body, pausing at her abdomen before dipping lower into the hot, wet folds of her most intimate flesh.

He had touched her like this, and he knew what she liked. One finger dipped inside her, then slid up to her clit, before traveling downward again. Her hips moved against his hand, as she silently told him how good it felt.

"Don't make me come like this," she whispered.

Reaching for his shoulder, she urged him on top of her. He looked into her eyes as she clasped his penis, doing what she had never done before, guiding him inside her.

His heart lurched in his chest, as her sheath closed around him.

"Rafe," she gasped.

"Right here."

He had thought about this moment for so long, but he hadn't known the reality would stun him.

They were both still for long moments, both of them overcome by what they had finally accomplished. Then she cupped his buttocks, urging him to move.

"Ah, God, Eugenia," he gasped as he did what they both wanted.

He started off with something approaching control. But the pace quickly become more urgent, more demanding as he took them both higher and higher.

"Oh Rafe, Rafe," she cried out, her movements becoming frantic under him as she sought her release.

Then she cried out, and he felt her contracting around him. He let go then, joining her in a climax that seized his whole body.

He collapsed against her. When he tried to move, she clasped him tightly.

He stroked his hand down her arm and knitted his fingers with hers. He wanted to tell her what making love with her had meant to him. But he'd never been great with words, so he turned his head, kissing her gently on the cheek.

He eased off of her, and gathered her in his arms, still hardly able to believe the reality of making love with her.

After long moments, he sensed she wanted to say something.

"What?" he murmured.

CHAPTER TWELVE

Eugenia hesitated. She knew she should simply enjoy this moment with Rafe. She had thought about making love with him so often, and they had finally done it. But she simply couldn't keep silent. In a barely audible voice, she said, "Rafe, what happened to the two of us after you left?"

She knew the moment she'd asked the question that she should have waited until they were on firmer ground.

A moment ago, they had been warm and cozy in her bed. When Rafe sat up and looked down at her, his expression had hardened.

Feeling suddenly exposed, she reached down for the sheet and carefully pulled it over her naked body. Pushing herself up, she said, "I wrote to you. But you never answered me."

"That's not the way I remember it. You were the one who didn't write. I . . . was in basic training and under a lot of stress. We'd agreed that I had to get away from New Orleans. I needed to know you were there for me, but you didn't answer me. And when I called your house, your mother said you weren't home."

She shook her head in confusion, trying to rearrange her thinking.

"I called, and I wrote you," he repeated, punching out the words. "By the time I came home on leave, you'd left for school in the East."

Perhaps he was reacting to the dumbfounded look on her face when he said, "What? Do you think I'm lying about it?"

"No," she whispered, wishing with all her heart that she had kept her mouth shut. But she'd been feeling so close to him that she'd thought they could finally talk. Or perhaps they should have done that before coming into the bedroom. But she'd been desperate to get him here.

Making love had been fantastic. Now it was all falling apart.

She watched him climb out of bed and start looking for the clothing he'd tossed onto the floor.

While he was getting dressed, she got up and pulled on her tee shirt and jeans, trying to figure out why he'd come into the bedroom with her. Because he'd seen the chance to get what she'd denied him all those years ago? She didn't want to believe that, but she couldn't ask him about it. Or anything else. Not now.

"I should go," he said.

She answered with a tight nod.

"But I don't feel comfortable leaving you alone."

"I'll be fine," she lied. Really, she was far from fine. In so many ways.

"I have to know you're safe. Is there someone you could stay with for a few hours?"

She struggled to get her equilibrium back. "I think I could go to a friend of mine. Larissa," she said. "She's a lawyer. With her own practice."

"How do you know her?"

"She—uh—handled my divorce. She's Larissa St. Stephens."

"Oh."

He didn't ask why she'd gotten married or divorced a couple of years later. Maybe he wasn't interested.

She turned away and reached for the phone.

"Ms. St. Stephens' office," Cora answered.

"This is Eugenia Beaumont."

"Hi. You're not having any problems are you?"

"Not legal problems. I've had some trouble here."

"I read about it."

"The detective I hired doesn't want me on my own. Could I come over there for a few hours?"

"Of course. Come on over."

"Thanks."

She put down the receiver and looked up. "All set."

"Good," he answered stiffly.

She and Rafe got back into his car, where she sat with her hands knitted together. They'd finally finished what they'd started years ago. She'd never been the kind of woman to jump into bed with a man. When she'd first met Rafe, she'd been cautious, and their sexual relationship had developed slowly. She'd been equally cautious with other men. But today, she'd wanted Rafe Gascon, and she'd pushed for what she wanted.

She thought she'd gotten it until she'd asked a question that had screwed things up between them again.

She gave him directions to Larissa's office, but that was the only thing she said to him.

He pulled into a fire lane in front of the office building that had been converted from an old plantation house. "I'll pick you up in a couple of hours,"

"What will you be doing?"

"Some stuff."

Since he apparently didn't want to talk about it, she got out. She was vividly aware of his eyes on her back as she walked toward the building.

Inside, she greeted Larissa's assistant, Cora, in the outer office.

"That was fast."

"I guess my bodyguard wanted some alone time."

"What bodyguard?" Larissa asked, poking her head out of her office. She was wearing one of her tailored suits and the high heels that looked so great on her but would kill Eugenia's feet. Her long blond hair was done up in a French twist. The two of them had gone to private school together and kept up their friendship into adulthood, which had made her a good choice for a lawyer when Eugenia needed to end a marriage that had been a mistake from the first.

"Well, it didn't start off as a bodyguarding situation. He's from a detective agency I hired after those muggings down near my restaurant."

"And now?"

"We found a nasty gris-gris on my doormat when we got home from the police station. And somebody was in the alley last night. We don't know who."

"Nice."

"So he doesn't want me to be alone."

"Wise. Come on in."

"You're not busy?"

"I've got a few hours between clients."

When they'd stepped into the office and closed the door, her friend embraced her. "I saw the news report of what happened in your restaurant. I'm so sorry you're in this mess."

Eugenia made a low sound. "Drawing in customers with a voodoo ceremony seemed like a good idea at the time. You know, blending New Orleans traditions."

"I would have advised against it."

"I know. That's probably why I didn't ask you."

"Was Villars murdered?"

Eugenia's face contorted. "We don't know yet why he died. Rafe will tell me as soon as he finds out."

"Rafe? You mean that sexy guy you used to hang out with?"

"Yes." Eugenia felt a rush of heat to her face. "He's with a firm called Decorah Security now. I hired them to investigate the mugging outside my restaurant. They sent him."

"How do you feel about that?"

There were so many things she could have said. She settled on, "He's good at his job." She plowed on. "He was on duty when Villars collapsed. Now the lead police investigator, Detective Cumberland, is giving both of us a hard time."

"I've had run-ins with Cumberland. He's a real bastard—with ambitions. That's a bad combination."

Eugenia nodded. Looking down, she ran her finger along the edge of her pocket.

"What else do you want to tell me?" Larissa asked.

"I guess you can see something's bothering me—besides someone dying in my restaurant."

Larissa waited and Eugenia finally said, "Rafe."

The lawyer's gaze sharpened. "What's he doing to you?"

"Not what you think." She swallowed hard before saying. "You know, when he went away, we each promised to write to the other."

"Uh huh."

"But he never did, and I was so hurt. Now he says I'm the one who didn't keep up the contact, and I have to believe he's not lying."

"And you've let yourself care about him again?"

"Yes," she whispered. "As soon as I saw him, I knew I still had feelings for him.'

"You have to talk to him. Try to figure out what happened."

"That's not so easy. You know he always felt like . . ." She raised one shoulder. "I guess you'd say that his social position put him at a disadvantage."

"Uh huh."

"That's changed. He's got a career. And he's good at his job, but there's still a barrier between us."

"Do you want to break it down?"

"Yes."

"Then you may have to be the one to do it."

"It's hard. And complicated because we're in the middle of this voodoo mess. Or a murder mess. I hope it doesn't turn out to be murder, but Cumberland is acting like it is."

She looked down at her hands. "Okay, I think I can't talk about this anymore."

"You should lie down, and try to get some rest. I've got a hideout in the back where I catch a power nap when I get a chance. You're welcome to use it."

"Thanks. I appreciate that."

Rafe had two people he wanted to visit and some other business to take care of. First on his agenda was Bennett Beaumont's restaurant on Chartres Street, a few doors down from the famous K-Paul's. Apparently Beaumont was thinking big.

He found a parking place a few blocks away and walked back. Unlike Eugenia, Bennett definitely wanted to trade on the family name.

Rafe stepped inside B. Beaumont's, looking around at the clubby atmosphere that featured dark paneling on the walls, captain's chairs with leather padding and burgundy carpet on the floor.

The man at the podium was wearing a suit. "I can give you a very nice table."

"I'm not here for a meal. I need to speak to Mr. Beaumont."

"He's in his office in the back. Whom shall I say is here to see him?"

"I'll just go back," Rafe said, striding down the hall without being invited. He knocked on the door that said, "Office," and walked in before the man inside had finished saying, "Come in."

Beaumont looked up. "Who are you?"

The restaurateur was a good-looking man, although he'd be better off losing about twenty pounds. A few years older than Eugenia, he had wavy brown hair, light eyes and a startled expression on his face. He sat on a leather couch in a nicely furnished room, a room that looked familiar. Rafe was working his way through that, when Beaumont spoke.

"Listen, buddy, tell me what you want or I'm making you get out of here."

"I'm Rafe Gascon, from Decorah Security."

"And?" Beaumont asked as he set down the glass of whiskey he'd been sipping. He looked soft, easy pickings for someone who had just issued a threat.

"We were hired to investigate the muggings occurring in the vicinity of Eugenia Beaumont's restaurant."

As he said the words, Rafe knew why the room looked familiar. He'd been here before—in a vision. This was where someone had put together the voodoo charm that had turned up on Eugenia's doorstep. And that someone was almost surely Beaumont.

Rafe had the satisfaction of seeing the man blanch, but he said, "That's none of my concern."

Rafe kept his gaze on the guy. "I think it is, and I think that if they continue, you are going to be sorry."

"Is that a threat?"

"It's a statement of fact."

"You'd better get out before I throw you out."

Rafe's voice was steady. "You and who else?"

He studied the man, watching him take in the reality that he was no match for his visitor.

Finally Rafe said, "If there's another mugging or another voodoo charm, you're in trouble."

He turned and walked back out the way he'd come, feelings of frustration and satisfaction clashing inside him. He knew now that Beaumont had made the gris-gris—as a scare tactic. But that didn't prove anything else.

Was Beaumont smart enough to heed Rafe's warning? He was half hoping the guy would try something again, because he was looking forward to teaching him a very serious lesson.

Rafe's next stop was the administration building at Tulane University.

He found Jillian Hargrave in her office in the back of the building, along a hallway painted institutional green. The blond young woman was dressed in a brown suit and beige blouse. With no makeup and her hair cut short, she looked like she was trying to fade into the room.

The moment he walked in, he saw the wary expression on her face.

"Ms. Hargrave?"

"Yes. What are you doing here?"

"You know who I am?"

"You were at the restaurant—when . . . that man collapsed."

"Yes."

"What are you doing here?" she asked.

Rafe studied her. She was obviously on edge. Because she had something to hide? Or because she was naturally wary?

"I'm interviewing the people who were there that night, trying to find out anything they saw that I might have missed."

"I didn't see anything unusual," she said quickly.

"Did you know Martin Villars personally?"

"No," she said, making Rafe wonder if she was lying.

"What's your interest in voodoo?" he asked.

"I find it empowering."

"In what way?"

"There are so many things you don't have control of in your life. It's a way to change the balance."

"So you believe it works?"

"As much as anything else."

He mulled that over, thinking that it reminded him of the person in the bayou who'd been contemplating the shrine. Could it be her?

"How do you know Calista Lacoste?"

He saw her hesitate. "I was walking past her shop and thought it looked interesting."

"So you're a customer of hers?"

"Yes. I've had some tarot-card readings."

Before he could ask another question, she said, "I'm really very busy. And I don't think I can be of much help."

"I'm sorry to bother you, but if you think of anything, give me a call." He pulled out one of his cards and handed it to her.

As he left, Rafe decided that he was going to poke into Ms. Hargrave's background a bit more. Could she have done something to Villars? She had kept her distance from him at the ceremony, but maybe that had been deliberate.

His mind played back the interview. He'd asked how she knew Calista, and she'd said they'd met at her shop. But, of course, they wouldn't have to know each other at all for her to have attended the ceremony. Yet she hadn't challenged that assumption. Instead, she'd come up with a plausible answer.

CHAPTER THIRTEEN

Rafe stopped at an electronics outlet and bought a couple of surveillance cameras, which he installed at the front and back entrances of Eugenia's property. He also called Pete Grady before he went back to pick up Eugenia and got several pieces of news he would have to share with his client.

When he phoned to say he was waiting out front, she came out almost at once. The strained look on her face made him want to sling an arm around her. With an effort, he simply escorted her to the car, then waited while she buckled her seat belt.

"Did you go looking for that voodoo altar?" she asked as he pulled away from the curb.

"No. I did a couple of other things."

She waited for him to elaborate.

"I had a conversation with your cousin Bennett."

Her gaze shot toward him. "Bennett, why?" she asked as he maneuvered the rush-hour traffic.

"I was thinking he could be the source of some of your problems."

"How?" she demanded.

"We already know he's jealous of your success in the restaurant business. I was wondering if he might want to throw a monkey wrench into your operation."

"He wouldn't!"

"That's what he says."

She sighed out a breath.

"But when I was in his office, I realized I'd seen it before —in that vision I had when I watched someone putting together the gris-gris we found on your doorstep."

Her breath caught. "That can't be true."

"I described the room to you. Leather sofa. Glass-topped coffee table. Oriental rug on the floor. It's the same room."

"I . . ."

"The rug was red with kind of rectangles all over the center and smaller ones of the same pattern in the border."

She caught her breath. "I've seen it in his office. It's a Bokhara."

"Unfortunately, that's not evidence I can take to the cops. But it means he was trying to harass you."

"Maybe he was taking advantage of the situation."

"You believe that?"

"I don't know."

"Well, I made it clear that he'd better not screw around with your business."

She snorted. "Right now, he doesn't have to. As we both know, the restaurant is closed," she said, as he came to a stop in the alley parking space.

He swallowed hard. "I have some good news and some bad news about that."

Her head jerked toward him.

"The good news is that you can get back in tomorrow morning."

Her head swung toward him. "What's the bad news?"

"Villars was poisoned with an old voodoo potion."

"Oh Lord."

"It's not your restaurant food, but Cumberland is looking at you and me."

The blood drained from her face. "But why?"

"He thinks we could have—pardon the expression—cooked something up together."

"How does he figure that?"

"Because of my history with him. I didn't tell you that when they thought I stole the brooch, Cumberland strip-searched me in Villars' office."

She caught her breath. "That's awful."

"Yeah. And then Villars found the jewelry in an antique chest."

"So you were cleared."

"But I was humiliated. And now maybe I asked you to help me get even."

"That's ridiculous. Why would I do something that would damage my business?"

"Of course you wouldn't. Which is why I'm thinking he won't be able to pin it on us."

She dragged in a breath and let it out. "When you say pin it on us, do you mean he'd plant false evidence?"

"I don't know. It depends on whether we think he planted that tracker on the car."

She looked sick. But there was more. He'd been waiting to hit her with something else, because the visit to Jillian Hargrave had triggered his own memory.

His tension mounted as he asked, "Do you know someone with a power boat called Windfall?"

Rafe took in Eugenia's confusion at the total change of subject.

"Windfall," she repeated.

"Do you know who might own it?" he pressed.

She was silent for several moments, then finally murmured, "I think it's Martin Villars'."

The information came as a shock. "Villars? You're sure."

"Why are you asking?"

"I was thinking about that vision I had—with the knife. Sometimes it's hard to process everything I experience." He didn't add that she'd totally taken his mind off the vision, and it wasn't until several hours later that he realized what he'd seen.

"How do you know about the boat?" he asked.

"I saw it when I was out at his country house catering a party. And you saw the boat in your vision?"

"Yes. I realized later that I'd seen the name. It was Windfall. Where's the house?"

"Near a wilderness area called the Jean Lafitte Preserve."

"How far from here?"

"Less than a half hour."

"I'm going out there to have a look around."

"We're going out there," she corrected.

"No."

"And why not?"

"I'm supposed to be keeping you out of danger."

"Villars is dead. He won't be there."

Rafe sighed. "He won't be there, but what if someone else is?"

"Like who?"

"How about the person who set up the altar." He used his cell phone to get the number for Villars' country home and dialed, then let it ring ten times, but there was no answer.

"Nobody's home," Eugenia said. "We can go ahead."

He wanted to tell her it wasn't her job to check out potentially dangerous locations, but he knew he'd only be wasting time. He had about three hours of daylight left, and he didn't want to use them up arguing with her.

"Okay. We'll stop by your house so you can put on rough clothes."

"What about you?"

"I'll change into jeans and a tee shirt."

They swung by her apartment, and they both went up and changed, Eugenia in her bedroom and him in the bathroom.

When Eugenia came out, she had a strange expression on her face.

"What?"

"I was thinking about Gertie—about how much she knew about voodoo."

When he said nothing, she added, "Do you think she could have put up that shrine?"

"I guess we have to figure it could be her. Did she have access to the house?"

"She certainly knew Villars. Maybe she'd know when he was out of town."

"Maybe we'll pick up some clues."

They headed for the house, which was in the town of Marrero that bordered Jean Lafitte. "

"It's not a real upscale neighborhood," Eugenia said.

"Why does he have a house out there?"

"I think he could get a lot of property for a good price, and it's next to the national park, which gave him privacy."

"Do you think Holly ever stayed in the house on her own? Or invited women friends out? Like maybe Gertie?"

"No idea."

"Was Gertie at the party?"

Eugenia thought back and caught her breath. "Yes."

"So she knew about the place."

"Yes, but it seemed more of a guy hangout. Maybe Villars used it for poker games or something."

"Why do you think so?"

"Because of the decor. I was thinking he might go out there without his wife—for men-only activities. I can't tell you anything specific. It was just a feeling I had."

"And you didn't have a chance to go exploring?"

"Sorry. I had a job to do."

He turned toward her, then back to the road. "How long ago was the party?"

"Three years."

"When you were just getting started. I suppose he got you for a very low fee."

She answered with a short laugh. "As a matter of fact, what he paid me barely covered the cost of the food. And I had to hire serving staff, too."

"You said he went for the daily special at dinner. But he didn't mind losing other people's money in an investment deal."

"Maybe he thought it was a sure thing."

"Tell me about the property."

"It's probably about a hundred years old, and when I was there, I saw a lot of renovation. New kitchen. New bathrooms. I think he picked it up from someone who had let it get run down—then had to sell at a low price."

"I wonder if he got the boat for cheap, too."

"It is called Windfall. Maybe he made a lot of money on a stock transaction. It looked out of place in the bayou. I'll bet the neighbors love him roaring around in it."

"Yeah, and the birds probably appreciated it, too."

"So what else can you tell me about the house?"

She thought for a moment. "The main floor has been opened up with a great room. I think there are three bedrooms upstairs. And," she stopped.

"What?"

"There was a locked room on the first floor."

"I wonder what was in it."

She shrugged.

"And the grounds?"

"I wasn't prowling around outside. There's an access road that's probably at least a block long. The grounds are nicely maintained around the house, but about fifty yards farther on, the bayou vegetation takes over."

Rafe was glad to discuss the property because he didn't want to discuss the two of them.

Eugenia had torn his heart out eight years ago, and he'd fought to focus his life in a different direction. Now he was wondering if somehow everything he'd been thinking for eight years was wrong. Although he wasn't prepared to talk about it, he was thinking that Frank Decorah might have intentionally thrown him and Eugenia back together.

The man who owned Decorah Security was a very odd character, when you came right down to it. He was strangely compelling. The men and women who worked for him all liked and admired him, but nobody knew much about him. Apparently he lived alone in a rural section of Beltsville, between Washington and Baltimore. As far as anyone knew, he wasn't married, and he had no significant other. Yet he seemed happy with his life. And he seemed to have a flair for matching men and women who belonged together. Like two of his other agents, Cole Marshall and Emma Richards, who had gone off on an assignment to rescue a kidnap victim on a slave ship and gotten married soon after.

Had Frank been playing matchmaker with them? And also with Rafe and Eugenia? Was he thinking that somehow they could figure out what had gone wrong eight years ago?

He turned his head and saw Eugenia staring at him.

"What?" she asked.

Because he wasn't willing to share his musings, he said, "I was thinking about the best approach to the Villars property. We'll park partway down the road and walk the rest of the way."

When they got to Marrero, he let her direct him. He

drove past first, seeing some houses close to the road, but the Villars home was far back and out of sight. After turning around, he pulled into a clearing along the access road, and they walked to the side of the gravel, weaving through vegetation as they approached the house.

"Does it look familiar?" Eugenia whispered. "I mean from your vision?"

He inspected the greenery on either side of them. "Yeah. Well, I'm seeing the same trees—cypress, tupelo, live oaks. And the Spanish moss. I don't know the names of the flowers, but I saw them before."

Cautiously, he walked across the soggy ground, stepping around a swampy area where duckweed floated. Eugenia followed, and he brushed saw palmetto and other shoulder-high plants out of the way.

When he could see the house through a screen of greenery he stopped.

"That's it?"

"Yes."

He hadn't seen the building in his vision. Now he took the time to run his gaze over the structure. It was about the size of a substantial two-story family home, with new windows, newly painted siding and a new brick walkway leading from a parking area.

"It's spruced up."

"He probably used local labor that he could get cheap."

He studied the dwelling for a few more moments. There were no lights on, and he didn't expect company, but he wasn't going to step out into the open until it was absolutely necessary.

"Do you know where the shrine was?"

"About thirty yards from the bayou, I think. Really, it looked like it was in the middle of nowhere."

They headed off to the right, circling around the house. He saw slow-moving water behind the building and also the dock. The speedboat was still moored there.

"The Windfall?" Eugenia asked.

"Yeah."

When he spotted the shack from the vision, he stopped short.

"That's it." He turned. "Stay back."

She gave him a fierce look. "I want to see it."

"Wait until I make sure it's all right."

He stepped to the edge of the vegetation and looked out at the cleared area. Then, cautiously, he approached the shed that he thought was being used as a voodoo shrine.

The door wasn't locked, and he carefully pulled it open. His breath caught. The shed was empty, except for the wooden shelf.

Movement behind him made him glance around. Eugenia had come up beside him

"There's nothing here."

"It *was* here. Someone's cleared it away."

He'd just closed the door again when the crack of a rifle shot broke the silence.

CHAPTER FOURTEEN

Rafe pulled Eugenia behind the shed, crouching down and dragging her with him.

"Who?" she whispered.

"I don't know. But we're getting out of here."

"You have your gun?"

"Yeah, but shooting someone while we're trespassing might be a bad idea."

As she made a sound of agreement, he looked back the way they'd come, not liking the stretch of open ground between them and the cover of the thick vegetation.

With the shed blocking the shooter's line of sight, he pointed toward a tupelo tree that had been left when the land was cleared.

"I'm going to create a diversion. You crouch over and run to that tree."

"What about you?"

"I'll follow."

He looked around and found a couple of baseball-sized rocks on the ground. Picking them up, he heaved one into the underbrush.

Immediately the shooter aimed at the sound and fired.

"Go," he whispered to Eugenia.

She took off for the tree.

He heaved another rock, then followed Eugenia, making it to the tree before the shooter realized he'd been suckered and fired toward them again.

Eugenia gave him a panicked look when he joined her behind the trunk.

Turning, he saw a dark-haired man holding a rifle. The guy was dressed in camouflage pants and a jacket.

Eugenia followed his gaze and gasped.

"You know him?"

"He was here when Villars had the party. He didn't have a gun then. And he was wearing a nice golf shirt."

"Who is it?"

"I don't know. What are we going to do?" She gulped. "I could stand up and say "Hi." Maybe he remembers me."

"And what are you doing sneaking around now?" Rafe searched the vicinity for an escape route. The bayou was twenty yards in back of the tree. "We're going into the water."

"That's dangerous."

"You have a better idea?"

"No."

He took her hand, ducking low as he led her toward the dark, slow-moving water.

When she hesitated on the bank, he pulled her in, staying

close to the side where the weeds were thick as he moved farther from the house, hoping the tall grasses hid them. He'd thought they'd gotten away until a shot hit the water about a foot from their hiding place.

"Take a breath and hold it, then get the hell under. Go with the current."

When she did, he followed her underwater, moving away from the Villars property.

He stayed below the surface as long as he could, then came up. Beside him, Eugenia was already gasping for air, her hair streaming around her face. They kept moving, and after about five minutes, Rafe lifted his head just enough to see if the man was following.

He'd stopped along the bank and was staring in their direction, but this time he apparently didn't see them through the weeds.

Praying that they weren't going to run into an alligator or a cottonmouth, Rafe kept putting distance between himself and the shooter.

When he reached another dock, he went under it, coming up on the other side.

"I guess we made it to someone else's property," he said.

"Thank God."

He was about to climb out of the water when he spotted a gator gliding toward them.

"Get behind me." As she complied, he picked up a piece of driftwood floating under the dock and whacked the creature on the snout.

The reptile turned around and swam in the other direction.

Eugenia stared at him, wide-eyed. "Good thing you saw him coming."

"Yeah."

"Could you have shot him?"

"My gun would have fired, but that guy who's after us would have heard."

"Right."

He started to hoist her out of the water, then looked up to see the man he'd just mentioned hurrying along the bank.

"Stay down," he whispered.

She followed his gaze and did as he asked, huddling under the water.

Rafe drew his Sig and shook the water out of the barrel, waiting tensely, but their pursuer kept going along the bank. When he was a hundred yards farther on, Rafe motioned to the underbrush about thirty feet from the water.

"I'll go first. If I make it, you come on."

She made a muffled sound as he climbed out and sprinted for cover, his shoes squishing so loudly that he was sure the guy would turn around. But the man with the gun kept walking, scanning the weeds and the surface of the water.

When Rafe motioned to Eugenia, she pulled herself up and made the same trip he had, flopping into the underbrush. They both lay still, watching the guy continue in the opposite direction.

Rafe reached for Eugenia, hugging her to him, thankful that they had both made it out of the water.

Praying that they weren't going to run into anyone else, he looked toward the house—hopefully, another vacation retreat. Cautiously, they both skirted the dwelling, and when nobody else came out with a gun, Rafe let out the breath he'd been holding.

"You look like a drowned rat," she said.

"Likewise."

It was getting dark by the time they reached the two-lane highway, then followed it back toward the Villars' property.

"You stay out of sight here," he said to Eugenia. "I'll make sure he's not guarding the car and come get you."

"What if he is?"

"I'll think of something."

He walked back toward the Villars house, once again staying in the trees to minimize being seen.

When he drew parallel with the car, he stopped short. In the gathering gloom, he could see the guy with the rifle about a hundred yards away, coming around a curve in the road.

Rafe had half a second to make a decision.

This time he wasn't so fussy about defending himself. He fired a warning shot, sending the guy ducking back around the curve in the road. Thinking he wasn't going to take a chance on another shot with a wet gun, he sprinted out of the trees, pushing the unlock button on the key as he ran.

By the time the guy poked his head out again, Rafe was already speeding away.

He heard shots behind him, but as far as he could tell, none of them hit the vehicle.

Eugenia had started up the road. She stopped short when she saw him, and he lurched to a halt, throwing open the passenger door.

"Get in."

She jumped into the vehicle and slammed the door as he took off down the two-lane highway.

"I heard gunfire," she gasped out. What happened?"

"The guy was coming down the access road," he answered as he put distance between himself and the Villars house.

"And you did what?"

"Fired once in his direction, then made a dash for the car."

She sucked in a sharp breath. "You could have gotten hit."

"But I didn't."

"Do you always take that kind of chance?"

"Only when I'm out in the bayou country with a rental car anyone can trace if they get a look at the license plate."

"I didn't think of that. Could he identify you?"

"At that distance when it was almost dark? Probably not. He saw us closer up back at the shrine."

"You think it's his?"

"I don't know," he answered as he pulled into a strip mall.

"Where are you going?"

"Drugstore. Wait for me."

Inside, he ignored the stares of the locals as he bought a couple of towels and a couple of tee shirts and sweatpants. His next stop was a nearby gas station, where he handed Eugenia a towel, a pair of sweatpants and a tee shirt.

"Go in the ladies room, dry off, and change your clothes. I'll be in the men's room."

They separated, and he stepped into the adjacent room,

where he locked the door and got out of his wet clothing. Then dried his hair and body before putting on the dry clothing.

"Can you hear me?" he called to Eugenia through the wall.

"Yes."

"Don't leave your wet stuff. We'll put it in the drugstore bag."

They both emerged five minutes later, looking more presentable.

She stuffed her wet clothing into the bag along with his, and he headed back to the city.

"Sorry about that," he said.

"Not your fault."

"I should have considered that the place might be guarded."

"Why should it be?"

He shook his head. He didn't know, but he was going to find out.

She cleared her throat. "That guy—I thought he was one of the guests when we catered the party out there. He didn't look quite so creepy the last time I saw him."

"Yeah."

When they reached her street, he pulled around back. As they'd driven into town, he could feel her withdrawing from him.

"Thanks for the . . . adventure," she said as he pulled up by the door to the courtyard.

"You're sure you don't want me to stay?"

"No."

"Let me check your apartment before you go in."

She answered with a tight nod, and he made a quick run through the rooms, seeing the bed where they'd made love.

When he came back out, she was standing stiffly by the door.

"All clear. You're sure you'll be okay?"

"Yes."

"If you have any problems, you've got my cell number." He stopped as he remembered the phone was ruined. "Well, as soon as I replace it."

"Yes."

There was nothing more to say at the moment. She disappeared inside, and he returned to his car. He understood why she might not want to spend time with him. But he wasn't planning to let her fend for herself. He was going to be around here—watching her place. From a distance. Because he wasn't going to give into temptation again the way he had earlier. He'd had no business climbing into bed with her. As far as he was concerned, he'd taken advantage of a woman who was emotionally off balance.

Maybe that impromptu swim had helped him get his priorities straight. But that didn't mean he wasn't going to protect her.

Rafe went back to his B&B to take a quick shower and clean and oil his gun. Then he replaced his phone and also bought a couple of burner phones that couldn't be traced. Finally he told Eugenia that his phone was back in service.

Next, he scoped out the vicinity of Chez Eugenia and decided his best move was to station himself in the courtyard of an empty building across the street. From there he could

use his portable hot spot to do some research while he moni-
tored the surveillance cameras he'd installed.

When he was finished with his preparations, he called
Pete Grady.

"You want an off-duty job?" he asked.

"Doing what?"

"I don't want to leave Eugenia home alone. I'm camping
out in a courtyard across the street, but I can't be here all the
time."

"And you want me to spell you?"

"Yeah, if you can do it."

"What are you paying?"

"How about thirty dollars an hour?"

"That's fine."

Rafe considered asking if there was any more information on Cumberland's witch hunt but decided against it,
figuring that if there was anything new, Pete would
tell him.

As soon as he'd secured his friend's services, he pulled
out one of the burner phones and called the Villars country
retreat, waiting with his breath shallow to find out who would
answer.

After two rings, someone picked up.

"Villars residence."

"Who am I speaking to?"

"Who wants to know? This number says it's unavailable."

"Because I'm making confidential calls. This is Mr.
Villars' lawyer, and I'm trying to locate some of the people
mentioned in his will. Who are you?"

"Carl Fortuna."

"Well, you may be in luck. I'll get back to you shortly. Can I have an address?"

Fortuna gave the address of the Villars property.

"You live on the Villars premises?"

"Yes. I'm the caretaker."

"I tried to call a few hours ago. Where were you?"

"At the store getting groceries."

Too bad, Rafe thought. If he'd known the guy was there, he could have kept Eugenia away.

The man was speaking again. "You think there's something for me?"

"Mr. Villars was very generous with his bequests. There may well be something for you." He cleared his throat. "I'm wondering if there's been any trouble out there."

"Why do you ask?" the guy demanded, his voice sharp.

"Sometimes people read death notices, and if they think a house is empty, they may try to break in."

"Well, I'm on the job here."

"Okay. Thanks."

He hung up. At least he had a name he could check out.

He did a search on Carl Fortuna and discovered that he had a rap sheet. Misdemeanors like drunken driving and public brawling. And one two-year stint for breaking and entering.

Why had Villars hired someone like that to watch over his property? Was he hiding something out there? Maybe Villars had been the one dabbling in voodoo, and he didn't want anyone to know about it.

He probably couldn't solve that mystery without going back. And now Fortuna would be on the lookout for intruders. Which left the question of why he'd lied to the lawyer about the recent incident out at the property. Maybe he'd thought he'd hit Rafe or Eugenia—and he didn't want to be associated with the death if a body turned up.

Rafe left those speculations on the back burner because there was one more piece of business he had to take care of.

The ME had released Martin Villars' body, and he wanted to stop in at the funeral home and see who else showed up and how they were behaving.

He dressed in the one dark suit he'd bought, along with a white shirt and subdued tie, a far cry from the outfit he'd worn on the trip to bayou country.

Villars was at the Medford Funeral Home, outside the central city. Rafe drove over and found about twenty-five cars in the lot. The building had once been an antebellum mansion. It had been renovated and beautifully landscaped. The private reception room was adorned with rich antiques, polished parquet floors and an enormous rug that looked like it had come from a Middle Eastern palace.

This being New Orleans, four black jazz musicians in dark suits were over in one corner playing somber funeral music. A nice touch, Rafe thought.

He looked across the crowd and saw the open casket. It looked like top-of-the-line oak.

When he walked over, he saw Villars cradled in gray velvet, dressed in a white suit with a white shirt and red tie. With a little subtle color in his cheeks, he was looking a lot better than the last time Rafe had seen him.

Holly Villars was nearby, dressed in a more sedate black dress, accented with a long string of pearls. She was talking in low tones to guests who had lined up to pay their respects. Instead of joining the line immediately, Rafe turned to survey the crowd. It appeared that many of Villars' associates from the business community had turned out. Although Calista was absent, most of the people who had been at the voodoo ceremony had come.

Gertie and Martha were standing by the refreshment table. He saw they were talking to Jillian Hargrave, dressed in the same unattractive suit she'd worn at work. It seemed designed to make her fade into the woodwork.

Rafe drifted over, wondering if they were three conspirators discussing a successful murder, but he couldn't get close enough to hear their conversation without being obvious.

Nearby was an open bar, and many guests had drinks in their hands. Others had plates of food. Rafe got himself a glass of club soda so he wouldn't look out of place.

Quite a send-off, he thought. First class and very expensive.

The atmosphere was sedate for a wake, respectful of the dead man, and Rafe couldn't help thinking how different the atmosphere was here than at the voodoo ceremony where Villars had died.

He felt the hairs on the back of his neck prickle. Glancing up, he spotted Cumberland watching him. He gave the cop a casual nod before turning away to greet Holly.

"You're that detective friend of Eugenia's," she said.

"Yes."

"You tried to save Martin's life, and you were kind to me after the EMT's wouldn't let me go with him to the hospital."

"I know it had to be awful for you. How are you doing now?"

"It's hard, but I'm coping." He saw her face harden. "If it wasn't for that slut of a voodoo priestess, he'd still be alive."

Rafe wasn't sure what to say. He hadn't seen Holly's animosity to Calista at the restaurant, but he supposed it might be the result of Villars' death now.

"Sorry," she murmured as she caught his reaction. "I shouldn't blame her."

"It's understandable," he answered.

Because others were waiting to speak to the widow, he stepped aside, making way for an older woman in a dark blue dress.

To his right, he saw Jillian bypass Holly and go to the other side of the coffin where she paused to stare down at Villars with an expression that could have been a mixture of relief and satisfaction before walking to the door and leaving.

She crossed paths with someone else coming in. Rafe went very still when he saw it was Eugenia, looking lovely in a simple navy dress, high heels and an upswept hairdo.

When she found him in the crowd, their gazes locked.

His heart turned over. He wanted to go to her and ask if she was all right, No, he wanted to take her away to some private place where they could try to resolve the conflict between them. She'd hurt him, and he'd been afraid to let her do it again. Now he was willing to risk it—risk anything if he could have her back.

That realization slammed into him as though he'd been hit in the chest with a baseball thrown by a major-league pitcher. For a moment, he couldn't breathe.

Then he regained his equilibrium. Eugenia was in danger. He was going to find out why and make sure nothing happened to her. Then they could resolve the very personal conflict hanging over them.

She didn't move for long seconds, and he wondered how she was reacting to him. Then she headed for the two older women who had been at the voodoo ceremony.

CHAPTER FIFTEEN

Because Eugenia had a busy week ahead, she was able to focus on getting her restaurant back in shape to open again.

Still, she couldn't help thinking about Rafe Gascon. After her conversation with Larissa, she'd been all fired up to speak to him about what had really happened eight years ago. Each of them had thought the other was at fault, and if they could have a rational discussion about it now, maybe they could get at the truth. Then he'd sidetracked her, and she'd put the personal discussion on hold.

Still, she kept thinking about how they'd gotten messed up when he'd gone into the army. And the more she thought about it, the more she was starting to form a theory about what had happened, a theory she didn't much like. What if her mother had deliberately broken their lines of communication? The idea made her sick. But if it were true, Mom would never admit it.

Knowing she had to let that go for the moment, she took a serious tour of the restaurant interior, making mental notes of what had to be done. Unfortunately, there was more than she'd thought from her first cursory inspection when she'd gone in to get the knife.

While she was emptying the trash out back, Jake Conrad, a reporter from Channel Six showed up.

"So you're back in business."

"Almost."

"I'd like to talk to you about the incident here the other night," he said.

"You mean on camera?"

"Yes."

She looked down at her grimy tee shirt and jeans. "Um, probably not this minute."

He grinned. "I'm not here to embarrass you in front of your fans."

"Fans?"

"You have a lot. The station's gotten a lot of calls about when you're going to reopen."

She had, too, and she'd put an announcement on her Facebook page.

"I'd like people to understand what happened here, and to find out your future plans."

She glanced at her watch. "I'm not open for business today, but if you could come back this evening, we could talk in the dining room."

"That would be perfect."

"Will it be live or taped?"

"Why don't we tape at ten, and I can get you on the eleven o'clock evening news?"

When he left, she wondered what she'd been thinking by

agreeing to talk on the record. But the advantages to her were obvious. She could show that she was back in control of her business and that she was looking forward to welcoming customers again.

Quickly she called some of her most reliable staffers and told them she'd pay them double their salaries if they could come over right away and help her get the restaurant in shape for business.

While she worked, she thought about questions the reporter would probably ask and tried to come up with the right answers. Practicing made her feel more confident.

Miraculously, by ten, the restaurant looked like the disaster had never happened. And her sous-chef had even managed to make a selection of hors d'oeuvres for the reporter and his crew.

She didn't even look too bad in her blue silk blouse and long black skirt. You'd never even know her heart was racing.

She gave herself one more glance in the mirror, patted her hair, and stepped aside to let Conrad in.

"I don't suppose you're going to share your questions with me ahead of time," she blurted.

He grinned. "Oh, it will just be the usual stuff. It will be fun."

She laughed. "I think your idea of fun and mine may differ somewhat."

Conrad and his crew conferred, and they decided she should stand at the side of the room, next to the antique sideboard she'd liberated from her mom's attic.

The reporter started with a recap of what had happened a few nights earlier, and she couldn't dispute the facts. But they certainly didn't make her look like she'd been making good decisions.

"So why did you allow a voodoo priestess to hold a ceremony in your restaurant?" he asked.

"As you noted, there was a lot of interest in coming to her ceremonies—in what my customers considered a safe environment."

"But one of them ended up dead."

"Yes, that's very unfortunate. And I'm so sorry it happened. But as far as I can see, it had nothing to do with the voodoo ceremony."

"Would you host a voodoo ceremony again?"

"Perhaps, but really, I think the main attraction of my restaurant is the food. I hope I'm upholding the long New Orleans tradition of excellent cuisine."

She went on to mention some of the dishes she featured. And Conrad even tried one of her boudin balls on camera and told everyone how delicious it was. By the time the interview ended, she was sure she'd done herself some good.

Apparently she was right. The next night, she had more customers than on any Saturday in memory. And she was up early in the morning the next day so she could go down to the wholesale markets to buy produce, meat and fish for Sunday.

The crush continued. Every table was filled, and she was taking reservations way into the next month.

But the biggest gratification came from the comments diners were making when she stopped by their tables to see if they were enjoying her cuisine. Everyone she talked to raved about her combination of Cajun specialties and down-home

Southern cooking. Several even suggested that she publish a cookbook.

The praise didn't turn her head. She was smart enough to know that it would take more than a few weeks of notoriety to firmly establish Chez Eugenia again in a town full of great restaurants.

But it looked like success was in her grasp. And so far there were no more muggings, probably because Rafe was still on duty.

That made her glance across the street to the courtyard she knew he was using. He hadn't spoken to her since they'd parted after their bayou swim, but she knew he was there. She could have told him she didn't need the services of Decorah Security any longer, but she thought it would be better to wait until the Villars case was resolved.

With a little pang, she walked back inside the restaurant kitchen, trying to put Rafe out of her mind. He'd come back to New Orleans and turned her world upside down. Now she silently admitted that she wanted him back in her life, and she wondered how that was going to happen. What if she tried to tell him her theory about her mother? Would he listen or walk away from her? That possibility made her throat constrict, but she told herself she could go on without him. She'd created a place for herself in the New Orleans restaurant scene, and she'd have the satisfaction of knowing she could make it in a highly competitive field—ignoring the aching gap in her personal life.

Over the next few days, nothing changed. Rafe was still across the street, and she was working hard at her chosen profession. Thankful that Wednesday was her day off, she took a nap in the afternoon. Refreshed, she decided she might as well use the time to bake some of her special sweet potato pies.

Before going into the restaurant, she stopped in the courtyard and looked across the street. Someone was over there. Either Rafe or that friend of his, Pete Grady, who had apparently agreed to take over some of the bodyguard duties.

Her chest tightened as she thought about going over there. And what? Taking some food like she'd done when she and Rafe had been teenagers?

Instead she went into the restaurant kitchen and started getting out what she needed to make the pies.

Just after it had gotten dark outside, she heard a trash can rattle in the alley.

Her gaze shot to the window. It was too dark for her to see anything. But she was clearly visible in the lighted kitchen.

There were no blinds back here. To cut down on her vulnerability, she crossed to the light switch and dimmed the overheads.

Was it Rafe out here? He wouldn't come over here without knocking on the door, would he?

If she went out the front, she could cross the street to where he was watching the restaurant. But what if someone was out front, too? Feeling trapped, she got out a butcher knife and laid it on the stainless steel counter beside her workstation. She'd been scrubbing sweet potatoes, but she went very still as she listened intently for more sounds outside. And now she was kicking herself for not bringing her cell phone into the kitchen.

When it sounded like somebody was trying to turn the lock, she grabbed the knife and prepared to defend herself. In the next second, the door burst open, and she gasped as her cousin, Bennett, came flying into the room and landed with a thud on the kitchen floor. Rafe was right behind him. He hauled him to his feet and whacked him with the side of his hand, drawing a gasp from him.

It must have been some kind of martial arts move that had Bennett howling in pain.

"Stop doing that to me."

"Yeah, I'd better stop before I do some real damage."

"What's going on?" Eugenia gasped out. As she turned on the light, she almost choked on the overpowering odor that had followed the men into the room.

"So you think your cousin is your friend?" Rafe made an angry sound. "I thought at least the bastard would be smart enough to stay away from you after our little chat. But apparently he couldn't deal with your surge of success. He was out back dousing your trash with charcoal lighter fluid. I saved him from getting arrested for arson."

Bennett gave him a defiant look. "It's your word against mine."

"Oh yeah?" Rafe gave the man another karate-type chop, then slammed him against the commercial refrigerator.

Her cousin must have seen the fire in Rafe's eyes because he abruptly stopped protesting his innocence.

"I'd like you to explain exactly what you were thinking," Rafe said.

Bennett folded his arms across his chest. "I thought the voodoo murder had finished her. Then she did that big whoop of a TV interview, and suddenly everybody was coming here again."

"And that was too much for you?" Rafe asked, his voice deceptively even.

"Listen, I've been working my butt off getting restaurant reviews. Pulling in customers. And she comes to town and starts taking everything away from me."

"It has nothing to do with you. I went to L'Academie de Cuisine in Bethesda, Maryland—one of the top chef schools in the country. Then I came home and opened a restaurant. I wasn't trying to compete with you. I was working hard to make a success of myself."

He made a snorting sound. "You've got your fifteen minutes of fame."

"If that's all you think it is, what are you worried about?"

Bennett didn't answer.

Rafe gave him a dark look. "When her success threatened you, you arranged to have a couple of people mugged outside her restaurant."

"Nobody got hurt bad. Just roughed up a little."

"That's just great. So kind of you." Rafe put his thumb and finger on her cousin's neck, and he screamed.

"Don't. Please."

"You're lower than a worm. Why are you here when I warned you to stay away from her?"

"I thought you'd gone."

"You bastard. So you waited until you thought she was unprotected." Rafe snorted. "Did you slip something into Martin Villars' drink?"

"Of course not! I wouldn't kill anybody. I wasn't even here that night."

"Except that you came over later and left that voodoo charm."

The man made a strangled sound. "You can't prove that."

"Maybe not. But I know it."

"But I wouldn't kill anyone," he repeated.

"You could have killed Eugenia tonight."

"No. She would have seen the smoke and flames and gotten out the front."

"Sure. Unless she'd passed out from smoke inhalation." Rafe regarded him with a murderous expression on his face.

"I want a lawyer," Bennett said. "You can't prove anything."

Rafe answered with a bark of a laugh. "As it turns out, I can. I installed cameras outside Eugenia's restaurant. You're the star of the current show. Maybe we should send *that* to Channel Six."

"No," Bennett shrieked.

Rafe glanced at Eugenia. "Do you want to put him on TV?"

"It's tempting, but I don't need any more questionable publicity."

"What about prosecuting him?"

She took her lower lip between her teeth. "What alternative do we have?"

Bennett gave a pleading look. "If you let me off, I'll

promise not to do it again. Or anything else that would hurt you."

Eugenia thought about it, and looked at Rafe. "He's my cousin."

"You trust him?"

"Not anymore. But you have the video you can use if we need to."

"He didn't listen to me last time."

Bennett broke into the discussion again. "Please. I promise to keep away from you."

She fixed her gaze on him. "You're going to sit down and write a confession, which Rafe will witness. And you will give a ten thousand-dollar contribution to a charity that helps disadvantaged children in the city."

"Yes. Of course."

"Eugenia will want a letter from the charity stating the contribution," Rafe added.

"Yes. I can ask them for that," he agreed immediately.

"Write down that you ordered the muggings and that you tried to burn the restaurant down," Rafe said.

"No. I was just setting her trash on fire."

"Okay, write that."

Bennett sat down at the table against the wall, and Eugenia brought over pen and paper. When he was finished, they both read what he'd written, and Rafe witnessed it.

"Now get out of here," he growled.

Bennett beat a fast retreat, and Rafe turned to Eugenia. "I hope we're not making a mistake."

"He's family."

"He's a snake."

She sighed. "But I feel sorry for him."

Rafe shrugged. If she was determined to take this course, he wasn't going to waste his breath on arguing.

Besides, they had more important things to discuss.

She beat him to it by saying, "You put up cameras without telling me? Why?"

"I wasn't going to leave you unprotected."

"Okay." She was silent for several seconds. "It looks like you solved the problem I hired Decorah Security to investigate."

As he heard those words, his heart stopped, then started to pound in double time. Was she telling him it was all over between them again?

He began to speak so quickly that it took a moment for his brain to catch up with his mouth. "There's still Cumberland's investigation hanging over us. He's still trying to prove we conspired to kill Villars."

"That's crazy."

"That hasn't stopped him."

She closed her eyes for a moment. "What can we do about it?"

"We can figure out who really killed him."

"How?"

"I want to get into his house and go through his stuff. But I can't do it if Holly is home. Can you get her out of the house?"

"How?"

"Well, you do feel bad about what happened to her husband. Is there somewhere you can offer to take her?"

Eugenia thought about it. "You talked about her husband's antique business. I can ask her out for coffee and tell her I'm looking for some new restaurant furnishings—and would she come with me to some of the shops on Royal Street." She made a snorting sound. "Not that I could afford anything in any of those places."

"But if you can get her to go with you, I can search the house in town."

He pressed his hands against his sides, wondering what he was going to do or say now. Maybe he had to be content that she still wanted to work with him.

"When should I call her?"

"As soon as possible. You're free during the day, right?"

"Except for cooking."

"Well, can your sous-chef handle most of that for one day?"

She nodded, then looked at her watch. "It's too late to call Holly now."

"Do it tomorrow morning, and let me know what you set up."

She cleared her throat. "I didn't thank you for catching Bennett."

"No problem," he answered, thinking there would be a very nice way to thank him and trying to get the thought of kissing her out of his mind.

CHAPTER SIXTEEN

The call from Eugenia came at ten a.m. "I'm picking Holly up and going to a café on Royal Street. We should be out for about an hour and a half."

"Great." He thought for a moment. "I'll have my phone on vibrate. If she wants to come home earlier, call me."

"Okay."

Rafe had come prepared. He'd studied the Google Earth image of the house so that he knew the exterior layout. He had found an old magazine article online that showed pictures of the interior. To complete the preparations, he was wearing a uniform similar to that of the New Orleans meter readers, which he'd picked up at a shop not far from where he'd used to live.

Rafe drove to the Villars mansion in the Garden District and arrived before Eugenia. He was lurking around the corner when he saw the two women leave.

After waiting five minutes to make sure the coast was clear, he strolled up the block and into the manicured yard.

He paused near the meter, pretending to take a reading, then made his way around the back of the house, which was screened from the neighbors by bougainvillea trained up the fence.

He put on a pair of gloves, got out his lock picks and opened the back door. He was inside within two minutes and thinking that maybe Eugenia should suggest to the widow that she needed better security.

He got his bearings from the pictures he'd seen, then started with Martin Villars' home office, looking for evidence that would give someone a motive to murder the man.

As they drove to the French Quarter, Eugenia said to Holly, "I'm so glad you could come out with me. It must be strange not having Marin around after all these years."

"It is."

"How are you doing?"

The widow sighed. "As well as can be expected. There are so many details to take care of. You'd think the authorities would make it easy on a widow, but they really don't. I had to find our marriage certificate and Martin's birth certificate. And I need multiple copies of his death certificate."

"It sounds like a lot to pile on top of you. I'm so sorry that my restaurant was involved in his death."

"Oh, that's not your fault."

Eugenia thought about the poison that had showed up in the autopsy but wasn't going to mention it. And really, it *wasn't* her fault.

"I hope we can have a few relaxing hours together," she said.

"It was kind of you to ask me out. But don't you have work to do?"

"Nothing I have to take care of immediately."

Eugenia found a parking space near one end of "antique row," and they both got out and headed for the charming little coffee shop with an interior courtyard that she'd discovered a few years ago.

Rafe turned on Villars' computer and was easily able to get into his files, since the man had used his birthday for a password. He did a rapid search of various folders and downloaded financial information that he could read later.

Next he started searching the office, looking behind books in the shelves, feeling along the baseboards, turning back the Oriental rug to look underneath.

He'd been at it for half an hour when he turned back a corner of the rug in the Villars bedroom and found a loose floorboard. Carefully, he pried it up and reached inside, wondering what he was going to find. It turned out to be a wide flat book.

Pulling it out, he saw that it was a photograph album. And when he began leafing through the pages, his breath caught.

Each section was devoted to a different girl—some white and some light-skinned African Americans. All of them were pretty, with good bodies, and all of them looked to be between the ages of fifteen and eighteen. There were several pictures of each young woman, most of them naked and all of them in what were clearly bondage and S and M poses.

Many had been photographed naked, spread eagle on a brass bed. The bed in this room, Rafe noted as he looked up from the book. Another room was featured in several photos, and Rafe suspected that it was at the Villars vacation house. No wonder the man had wanted to keep his activities out there private. Did he and the caretaker do some of this stuff together?

He went back to the book. Sometimes the girl was standing shackled with her hands above her head, and there might be clear lash marks on her back or breasts. Or she might be sitting in a chair with her legs spread, perhaps masturbating. One girl was wearing only high heels and leaning over a table with a dildo sticking out of her rear.

Sometimes the subject might be wearing a garter belt or a bra designed to leave the nipples exposed. Sometimes her breasts were bound. In one shot, the girl was posed with a hood over her face and a riding crop handle poking at her sex.

There were some pictures that featured two girls, one whipping or fondling the other. It seemed that Villars had forced a lot of interesting activities on young women he had under his control.

Rafe turned the pages and stopped, the breath catching in his lungs. He knew one of the girls. It was a much younger Calista Lacoste, in a number of the poses similar to what he'd already seen. And in one picture, she was on her knees in front of a man, sucking his cock. The man in the picture was clearly Villars. Either he'd used a timer to get into position to take the shot or Fortuna had taken it.

Rafe had just seen that picture when his phone vibrated. Eugenia and Holly must be on their way back—early.

Christ! Did he have time to get out the back door, or did he need to use a window, he wondered as he stuffed the album under the back of his shirt and into his waistband so he'd have both hands free.

"I'm sorry I pooped out on you," Holly said as Eugenia pulled into her driveway. "It's just that I don't seem to have the energy I used to. Or maybe it's that I'm not sleeping so well, now that the other side of the bed is empty."

"I understand," Eugenia answered, hoping that Rafe had felt the phone vibrate and had the time to get out of the house. "Do you need any help?"

"No thank you. But I do appreciate your thinking of me."

"We'll have to do this again soon."

Eugenia watched the older woman climb her porch steps, open the door and disappear inside.

Was Rafe still in there? Eugenia didn't see him, but she didn't think he could have already left.

Rafe had raised the window to the porch roof when he heard the front door open. With a silent curse, he climbed out.

He could hear someone coming rapidly upstairs. Presumably Holly. Did she suspect that he might have been here?

He quietly closed the window, then flattened himself on the roof.

Looking out toward the street, he saw Eugenia standing beside her car, staring at him.

She pressed a hand to her mouth, then reversed directions and hurried back toward the house, where she rang the front bell.

The footsteps that had been heading toward the window stopped.

"Holly?" Eugenia called.

"Just a moment." Mrs. Villars walked back into the hall and started downstairs. Making a quick calculation, Rafe pushed himself to the side of the roof, and dived into a crepe myrtle tree, making the slender branches bounce and sway. When the tree stopped shaking, he swung down, made it to the ground and ducked into the bushes as the front door opened.

"Yes?" he heard Holly ask.

"I'm sorry to bother you, but did you happen to see what I did with my umbrella?" Eugenia asked.

"I don't remember seeing it. Are you sure you had it with you?"

"Maybe you're right. I may not have had it at all. Sorry to bother you."

"I do need to rest," Holly said.

"Sorry," Eugenia repeated.

When the front door had closed, she turned toward the

street, then stopped short when she heard Rafe rustling in the bushes.

He shook his head. "Go on; I'll meet you," he mouthed.

She gave a little nod and hurried back to her car.

Rafe waited for several minutes to make sure he was in the clear. Finally he crawled across the lawn, using as many bushes for cover as he could.

Praying that Holly had done what she'd said and lain down, he made it to the street and kept walking around the corner at a normal pace. He was wearing a uniform and a cap, he told himself. There was really no way of recognizing him from the back. He hoped.

He made it to Eugenia's apartment a few minutes after she did.

The look of relief on her face when she opened the door made his heart turn over. They might be at odds, but he knew that she cared about him.

He sat down heavily on the couch, and she studied his face. "You scratched yourself."

"In the crepe myrtle tree."

"Let me put something on it."

"Okay."

She disappeared down the hall and came back with a wash cloth and a bottle of antiseptic. She sat down beside him, closer than she'd been since they'd made love.

He tried not to think about that as she washed off the scratches.

"The second time you're patching me up," he said in a thick voice.

"Yes," she murmured. "This may sting."

"Better than getting an infection."

When she opened the bottle and poured some of the liquid onto a sterile pad, he smelled the pungent odor. And when she swiped it on one of the scratches, he winced.

"Sorry."

"It's okay."

She finished up the first aid and recapped the bottle. She was so close, her eyes on his lips. He wanted to kiss her. Maybe she wanted it too. But he had business to discuss with her.

"Thanks for going back and distracting Holly. She was right inside that room where I'd flopped onto the porch."

"Was it worth it? Did you find anything?" she asked.

"Yeah."

"Something that might be a motive for murder?"

"It might be."

She made an exasperated sound. "Are you going to tell me what it is?"

"It's kind of disturbing."

"You brought it?"

"Yes."

"Do I have to beg to see it?"

He sighed and pulled the photo album out from under his shirt and held it in his lap.

"What's that?"

"Martin Villars' little hobby."

"What?"

He swallowed. "He liked to get into S and M scenes with teenage girls.

"You're kidding."

"Unfortunately, no." He shifted in his seat. "This book is full of the very graphic pictures he took of them. In poses that aren't very nice."

"Can I see them?"

"In a minute. I want to explain one more thing."

She waited.

"One of the girls is a much younger Calista Lacoste."

Her eyes widened. "Oh my God. Let me see."

He handed over the book, and she drew in a sharp breath as she took in the first picture. Then she began flipping through the pages, obviously not looking at the photos in detail until she came to Calista. She sucked in a breath as she looked at the voodoo priestess.

"She looks like she's around sixteen."

"Yeah."

"How did she hook up with him?"

"I don't know."

"Would she murder him for this?"

He shook his head. "This was twelve years ago. Why wait so long?"

Eugenia reached for the book and flipped back to one of the pictures—of Calista and another girl, kissing and fondling each other.

"That other girl looks familiar."

Rafe studied the picture. "You think you know who she is?"

Eugenia kept looking at the photo. "I'm trying to imagine

her with a different hairstyle. Shorter. Blonder. And without glasses."

When he heard her breath hitch, he said, "You know who she is?"

"Jillian Hargrave."

"She was at the funeral home—and the voodoo service. Had she come to Voodoo Night before?"

"Yes."

"So she and Calista could have cooked something up together."

"Yes."

"What if he was blackmailing one or both of them?"

"That could be it." He laughed. "You'd think it might be the other way around."

"Calista's getting more known in the city. She might not want anyone to see the pictures. And what about Jillian?"

"She's a systems administrator at Tulane. I interviewed her there."

"How did she seem when you talked to her?"

"Closed up."

He went back to the book and flipped some of the pages. "The photos are dated. He was still doing it. The last pictures were taken only a few weeks before he was murdered. Maybe a more recent victim came after him."

"I hope Holly didn't know about this."

"She's not in any of the pictures."

"Why would she be?"

"Sometimes stuff like this is a husband-and-wife project. Or it could be like that football coach who molested boys in the shower and also brought them home for sleepovers. It's impossible to believe that his wife didn't know a thing about it."

She made a disgusted sound. "You could say Villars was a dirty old man. And a dirty younger one, too." A thought struck her, and she asked, "Are we going to tell Cumberland about this?"

"I'd rather not point the finger at anyone until we have more information."

"Is revenge or blackmail the only motives you've come up with?"

"I've investigated everyone who was in the room. As far as I can tell, the tourists were all what they seemed to be—people intrigued by the idea of attending a voodoo service in safe surroundings."

"If Calista didn't do it with Jillian, it could have been one of the people working for Calista the night of the ceremony. There were six of them."

"And one of the guys tried to run out."

"But apparently because he was worried about his illegal status."

Rafe cleared his throat. "Maybe we can get a better look at what happened the night of the ceremony."

"How?"

"I may be able to send myself back there."

She tipped her head to the side, keeping her gaze on him. "How?"

"If I have the right thing to touch."

"What?"

"You."

CHAPTER SEVENTEEN

Rafe watched Eugenia suck in a sharp breath. "How would that work, exactly?"

"I think I can take us both back to the night of the murder. If we're in the restaurant."

She glanced at her watch. "We can't do it now. The restaurant's open tonight. I should go down there soon and make sure the cooking's going okay."

If she thought she was going to get out of it, he disabused her of that notion. "Then we'll wait until you finish for the evening."

She considered the suggestion, then nodded.

"I was up most of the night getting ready for my breaking and entering gig. Do you mind if I catch some sleep on your couch?"

From her hesitation, she probably didn't want him sleeping in her apartment, but she didn't refuse.

He lay down and closed his eyes, and was out within minutes.

Eugenia tried to go through her regular routine, but it was difficult to focus.

First she kept seeing images from Martin Villars' private photograph album.

Would any of the girls in the pictures have gotten into a kinky relationship with the man if they'd had a choice? Perhaps, but would any of them have wanted their pictures taken doing the things he forced on them?

They were all young. All probably his victims. She tried to put herself in their places and shuddered.

Of course, she wasn't naive. She knew there were women who liked this sort of thing. But she had the feeling Villars hadn't given any of them a choice.

Had Calista been the one to seek revenge? But why now, after all these years? Judging from the way she looked in the pictures, they must have been taken at least ten years ago. Maybe he'd lost track of her, found her again, and made demands. Or maybe it was Jillian. If there was ever a woman who was trying to make herself unattractive to the opposite sex, it was her—and probably because the S and M stuff had damaged her.

Eugenia couldn't come to any conclusions, and she realized that speculating was only upsetting her. So she focused on the dishes she was cooking and went into the dining room periodically to chat with her guests. She'd always thought of herself as primarily a good cook, but now she saw that she'd taken on the status of celebrity chef, with customers eager for a few moments with her.

She got through the evening and supervised the cleanup of the dining room and the kitchen. When everyone had cleared out, she went up to the apartment. Rafe was sitting up on the sofa, running a hand through his hair.

"How are you?" they both asked at the same time, then both answered, "Fine."

"What is it that we're going to do, exactly," Eugenia asked.

"We're going to take ourselves back to the night of the ceremony and see what we can see."

"But we were both there."

"And watching Calista," he pointed out. "Plus I want to go back before she started her performance."

"How do we do it? I mean, with the knife and the gris-gris, didn't it take you somewhere without your being in charge of the trip."

"Yeah. But this time I'm focused on where I want to go, and I think if we work together, we can go back to the ceremony."

She could tell from the way he said it that he wasn't as confident as he'd like, but she wasn't going to challenge him. If they could prove that they hadn't murdered Villars, they could get Cumberland off their backs.

"Let's go down," he said.

"I'd like to take off my chef outfit first."

"Sure."

He waited in the living room while she went into the bedroom and opened a dresser drawer, looking for what to wear. If she was going to do something weird, she might as well be comfortable.

After taking off her cooking outfit and laying it over the arm of her chair, Eugenia pulled out a tee shirt and old sweatpants, and then scuffed her feet into a pair of well-worn moccasins. She'd talked to Rafe about his trips outside his own body, but she'd never participated in any of them. And she wasn't too keen on it now. But she understood that it might be the key to solving a murder case.

Unable to keep a shiver from traveling over her skin, she went out to face Rafe.

"Good choice," he commented as he took in her costume.

"Thanks."

They both descended the steps, and she unlocked the backdoor of the restaurant that she'd locked only a short while earlier.

"We should go into the room where it happened," Rafe said as he led the way to the front of the house.

He glanced around.

"What are you looking for?"

"Our best vantage point."

"I still don't quite understand this. Aren't you always in someone else's body?"

He dragged in a breath and let it out. "Yeah, but I'm going to see if I can do it differently."

"How?"

"Okay, we were both in this room before and when Villars died. Or, as you probably remember, I was 'away' for a few minutes."

"That's right. I wasn't thinking about the first time you touched the knife."

"I might have seen something if I'd been there."

"I was in the room the whole time," she pointed out.

"But you might not have realized what you were seeing."

When she nodded, he continued, "I want to go back, and I can use you as a touchstone and also use the room. We were both in the back. Let's go up to the front."

"You can change your perspective?"

"I hope so."

They both walked to the area where tables had been pushed back to make a stage area for Calista. Eugenia looked back toward where the audience had been. "Here?"

"I think it's the best place. I'm going to take us there, and we're both going to watch the people."

"Did your friend Pete know how long it would take for the poison to kill?"

"He thought about fifteen minutes."

"So we go a little farther than that fifteen minutes before Villars died."

She'd taken care of his scratches, but other than that they hadn't touched since they'd made love. When that image leaped into her mind, she felt her cheeks heat.

"What?"

"Nothing."

"I want you to focus on the period twenty minutes before Villars keeled over."

"I thought you were taking us there."

"It's better if we both do it."

He leaned a shoulder against the wall, and held out his arms. "Come here," he said in a thick voice.

"Is this a trick to get me close to you?" she couldn't stop herself from asking.

"No, but it's a side benefit."

He reached for her, pulling her into his embrace. She held herself stiffly for a moment before ordering herself to relax.

As she did, the room around her started to swim, and her skin began to tingle. She hadn't thought anything would happen, but she'd been wrong.

The restaurant had been empty when they'd come in, but she heard noise creep in around the edges. People laughing and talking. Then she gasped as the crowd flickered into existence. It was the scene from last Tuesday night, when she'd had fifteen people here, waiting for the voodoo ceremony to start.

She clung to Rafe, feeling like she might lose her way and never get back, until she felt his arms tighten around her and knew he would keep her safe.

Gradually the pounding of her heart subsided, and she was able to turn in his arms and observe the scene.

"Can the people see us?" she whispered, wondering if Rafe could hear her.

"No."

"What about us. I mean the us who were there."

"I see you across the room."

She shivered and did what she hadn't dared earlier. Her gaze flicked to the left, and she saw herself talking to one of the tourists who had showed up that night.

Gertie got up and headed for the ladies room before the ceremony started.

Then Holly, Villars' wife, stood and came over to the food table, which was only a few feet away from where Eugenia and Rafe were standing.

Holly looked right at them, and Eugenia's breath stilled. Could the woman see them?

Maybe she saw *something* but didn't know what it was.

She shook her head, then glanced around before putting several hors d'oeuvres on a small plate. Again she checked to make sure she wasn't being watched, before using her finger to push at the jewel on top of the large antique ring she wore. She flicked it aside and turned her hand over a bite-sized quiche. Drops of liquid fell onto the food. After pushing the jewel back into place, she carried the plate to the table where her husband was sitting. Once she'd set it down, she handed Villars the piece of quiche.

He popped it into his mouth, chewed and swallowed.

Eugenia couldn't hold back a gasp. "It's her. She did it. The poison was in that ring."

They stood where they were as the dancers and Calista came in, and they watched until Villars keeled over.

"Let's go," Rafe whispered.

The room swirled around them again, and they were back in the empty restaurant.

Eugenia's heart was thumping as Rafe's arms tightened around her.

"It's Holly. Oh Lord, I can't believe it's Holly," she breathed. "But we both saw her do it."

"Yeah, the grieving widow. I guess we read her wrong about her feelings for Villars."

"Everybody read her wrong—including Cumberland. Or I guess you could say, including her husband."

Eugenia pushed away from Rafe, pulled out a nearby chair and sat down heavily. "We have to tell Cumberland."

"Tell him what?"

"That we saw Holly put something on a quiche and hand it to her husband."

Rafe made a scoffing sound. "Oh sure. You think he's going to believe that we went back in time and watched the ceremony from a different angle?"

"Then what?"

"My talent works as an investigative tool, but it's not proof of anything. We have to get better evidence," he said.

"Or a confession."

"Why should she confess? We can't prove anything."

"I think I can get her in the right mood."

"Too dangerous."

"You have a better suggestion?"

"Now that we know it's not Jillian or Calista, I want to talk to Calista," he said.

"She's not going to like it that we know about her past."

"Probably not."

Eugenia stood up, but her legs were shaky. When she started to fall, Rafe caught her, wrapping his arms around her.

She'd clung to him while they went back to the scene of the crime, but this was different.

She'd deliberately kept away from him, struggled to

detach her emotions from him until they had a chance to sit down and talk, but now she wasn't able to do it any longer, especially since she'd watched his reaction to her statement that Decorah Security had done the job she'd hired them for. He had wanted a reason to stay close to her. That knowledge made her heart squeeze.

When she tipped her head up, he brought his mouth down to hers. Maybe he had intended it to be a reassuring kiss, but the moment his lips touched hers, she knew he wanted more, and so did she.

She trembled in his arms, running her hands over his back, his shoulders, gathering him closer, melting against him.

She wanted to ask what they really were to each other. But she wasn't going to make the same mistake twice. She wasn't going to spoil this by talking.

She heard herself make a small, needy sound, felt sparks flickering to every nerve ending in his body. He angled his head, first one way and then the other, greedy to give and take.

She could have pushed him away when he cupped her breast, stroking his thumb in a maddening rhythm back and forth across the hardened tip. But she didn't.

She began to move against his erection, frustrated that it was hitting her middle, not where she needed it. She shifted to press her clit against his thigh, unable to stop herself from trying to assuage the ache that had started deep inside her.

His eyes locked with hers, silently asking if she wanted to take this to its logical conclusion, and she answered with a small nod.

He yanked her sweatpants and panties down, before

setting her on one of the tables. Then he unzipped his fly, freeing himself. In the next moment, he was inside her, moving with an urgency that took her breath away. The intensity built quickly, carried by the strength of their emotions.

Reaching between them, he pressed his hand against her clit, giving her extra stimulation as he surged in and out of her.

He called out as he came, and she clung to him as she followed.

Afterwards, they held each other for a long moment, then eased apart, and both put themselves back together.

"I'm sorry, chérie," he said.

"If I hadn't wanted it, it wouldn't have happened," she heard herself admit.

She wanted to say more. But she'd gotten burned last time she'd brought up their shared past at the absolute wrong time.

Instead she said, "I think we have to talk to Calista."

"Yeah." He gave a harsh laugh. "She's going to love the conversation."

"Do we show her the book?"

"I think we copy the pictures and put the book away in a very safe place in case she decides she doesn't want anyone to know about her past.

"Good idea."

CHAPTER EIGHTEEN

While Rafe used the scanner and the computer to make and print out copies of the photos with Calista and Jillian, Eugenia washed up and changed from her sweatpants and tee shirt into jeans and a white silk blouse.

When he had put the pictures into a folder, they looked for a good place to hide the book.

Rafe unscrewed a heating vent, shoved it inside and put the cover back on. Then Eugenia called the voodoo priestess's cell.

Calista picked up on the second ring.

"Eugenia?"

"Yes."

"You're calling pretty late."

"We need to talk to you," she said.

"About what?"

"About Villars' murder."

Her voice turned sharp. "You think I'm involved?"

"No. We think we know who did it, but we need proof. Can we come over to talk to you?"

There was a long hesitation on the other end of the line. Finally Calista said, "Okay."

When they were in the car, Eugenia said, "I— uh— thought of something. The autopsy report said the poison was a voodoo potion. What if Holly got it from Calista?"

"I thought of it too and decided it was unlikely," Rafe answered.

"Because?"

"Because a voodoo potion would implicate Calista, so why would she want someone to use it at a ceremony she was conducting?"

"A good point."

"Holly probably wanted the cops to suspect Calista—and instead Cumberland's focused on us."

"Yeah."

They pulled up at a modest house in Gentilly.

The porch light was on, and when they rang the bell, the voodoo priestess came to the door quickly, wearing a pair of jeans and a mint-green cashmere sweater, an outfit that Eugenia had never dreamed of seeing on her.

She ushered them into a large living room.

The exterior of the house looked a lot like its lower-middle-class neighbors, but the interior had obviously been extensively modified to combine several small rooms into one, with a newly installed kitchen area at one side. The furnishings were modern, with interesting African accents like a six-foot-tall giraffe in one corner, wooden masks on the wall, and tall carved candlesticks.

"You said you think you know who killed Villars," Calista said. "Who?"

"It's complicated," Rafe said. "We should sit down and talk."

Her reaction was similar to Eugenia's when Rafe had put off showing *her* the book.

"Listen, you can't drop something like that on me and then not come clean with me."

"Let's sit down," Rafe said again.

He moved to a comfortable seating area with a sleek leather sofa and two chairs facing each other across a metal and glass coffee table.

Rafe and Eugenia took the sofa. Calista sighed and dropped into one of the chairs.

"We figured out why someone might want to get even with Villars," Rafe said and passed her the folder. As soon as she opened it and saw the first picture, she made a moaning sound.

"Where did you get this?"

Eugenia answered. "I got Holly out of the house so Rafe could search for evidence. He found a photo album hidden under a floorboard."

"And these are copies of some of the pictures? Where are the originals?"

"In a safe place."

"Are you trying to blackmail me?"

"No. You're not the only teenager in the book. There are at least two dozen more. In similar poses. And there's one pose of you and Jillian Hargrave together."

"Shit." She got up, walked away from them and stood with her back to them. "This is going to make Jillian sick."

"What about you?"

Instead of answering the question, she said, "Martin used to say Holly hated his play-time pursuits, but she couldn't do anything about it."

"Apparently she did."

"How do you know it's her? If there are dozens of women in the book, one of them could have gotten her revenge. I mean, Jillian was there that night."

Rafe cleared his throat. "It wasn't Jillian. Come back so I can talk to you."

She returned and sat in the chair, her expression angry.

"You can believe this or not. I have a talent for touching objects and getting visions from them."

Her eyes widened. "You? How? Why?"

"I don't know how or why. It's just something that's been with me since puberty. That gris-gris we brought to you last week. When I touched it, I got an impression of somebody making it. I mean I saw them doing it, but I didn't know who it was until I went to question Eugenia's cousin and realized I was in the room where it was put together"

Calista tipped her head to the side. "That's a talent more likely with the black folks."

"Maybe in your world. In mine, I know a lot of people who aren't black—with talents you wouldn't believe. But let's stay on topic. I took Eugenia back to the night of the ceremony, and we saw Holly put poison on Villars food."

"How?"

"Remember that big ring she was wearing? She moved

the stone aside and dripped something onto a piece of quiche."

"Clever," Calista muttered.

"Of course we can't use that as evidence, and by now she could have thrown the ring away."

Calista nodded.

"What do you know about Holly?"

"She came to me asking for voodoo lessons."

Eugenia sucked in a breath. "Did you give them to her?"

"I taught her some things about the religion."

"Did you teach her how to make poison?" Rafe said.

"No. But I lent her some books. They had old recipes." She gave him a direct look. "I make love potions and gris-gris, but I don't make poison."

He didn't know if he believed her, but he knew she hadn't killed Villars.

She kept her gaze fixed on him. "And in any case, I wouldn't have poisoned Villars. Her eyes were bright as she said, "There were some girls who hated what he did to them. At least one died of shame. And I know one killed herself. But not me. I found out that I liked it. Well, all except for when he made me do stuff with that creep, Carl Fortuna."

Eugenia grimaced. "His caretaker out at Marrero?"

"Yeah. You know him?"

"Not well. He was at a party I catered out there."

"Villars was one thing. Fortuna was another."

"You're saying you consented to your relationship with Villars?" Rafe asked.

"Not at first. Then I realized it turned me on, and I kept up the contact—on the proviso that I wouldn't have to see

Fortuna again. Villars met with me from time to time over the years, sometimes in town and sometimes at the country house. And he didn't always want to be the top. Sometimes he wanted me to dominate him, which I was glad to do. He could be very generous to girls who pleased him. He rewarded me by setting me up in my shop. I owe him a lot. There's no reason I would want to kill him."

She looked defiantly at the other two people in the room.

"That's why he had a locked room out there?" Eugenia asked.

"Yeah." His playroom.

Rafe leaned forward. "How did you meet him?"

"I was the protégé of a voodoo priestess named Denada. She thought Villars would like me. And he did."

"And what about Jillian?"

"She had run away from home and was living on the street. She did a lot of stuff for money. Villars was out looking for young tail and brought her home. When I found out her background, I convinced her to go back to her family. And she took my advice. Her parents were strict but well off. She stuck it out at home until she went away to college. When they died, she inherited a lot of money from them."

"You said you had no reason to kill him. What was her attitude toward him?" Rafe pressed.

"She hated him." Calista laughed. "She used her computer expertise to steal from him. She enjoyed making money disappear from his accounts. That was more satisfying to her than killing him."

Rafe nodded, thinking about the convoluted relationships among the people who had been at the voodoo ceremony.

"One more question," he said.

Calista gave him an inquiring look.

"There was a knife on the table at the ceremony. Where did it come from?"

She tipped her head to the side. "I thought." She stopped and looked at Eugenia. "You didn't put it there?"

"I thought it was yours."

"I'm guessing it was Holly's," Rafe said. "I think she put it there for symbolic reasons."

"Why?"

"She used it to kill a goat in a voodoo ceremony. I guess she wanted that extra juju. But that's not what we really need to worry about. We have to figure out how to get ourselves off the hook by trapping Holly into a confession."

A loud rap at the door made them all go rigid.

"Police. Open up."

CHAPTER NINETEEN

Calista looked at Rafe. "What should I do?"

"You have to open it, or they'll bust it down," he answered in a controlled voice.

When she opened the door, Detective Cumberland strode into the room, wearing his usual expensive suit and looking pleased with himself.

"Well, well. The nest of conspirators. What are you up to —trying to figure out how you're going to deflect my interest?"

"No," Rafe said, looking the man straight in the eyes and thinking he'd like to ask how the detective kept showing up everywhere they went. But he knew he wasn't going to get a straight answer.

"Then what are the three of you doing together?"

"We know that Holly Villars killed her husband, and we're discussing what to do about it."

Cumberland laughed. "The distraught widow? And what is her motive, pray tell?"

"She was angry about her husband's extramarital activities." Rafe looked at Calista. "I'm afraid you're going to have to show him the pictures."

Her face had gone chalk white, but she picked up the folder from the table and handed it to Cumberland."

"What is this?"

"It's pretty clear," Rafe said.

Cumberland's eyes bugged out when he saw the photographs, including the one of Calista with Villars.

"What did you do, fake these?"

"Look at Calista's face in the photos. These pictures are ten years old. It's like saying Obama's mother faked his birth announcement in the Honolulu papers. Nobody planned a conspiracy years in advance."

Rafe could see that Cumberland conceded the point. "Then where the hell did you get these?"

Rafe kept his voice low and calm. "Villars forced Calista and dozens of other girls into an S and M relationship with him against their will. We found the pictures in an antique chest that must have belonged to Villars."

Neither woman in the room spoke up to correct him.

"Apparently it was Villars' sick little hobby to dominate young woman, and his wife didn't like it. Which is why she killed him."

"You have proof of this?" the detective asked.

"No."

Cumberland snorted. "Then this is all a story to throw me off the track."

"No," Rafe said. "I saw her put the poison in a miniature quiche and hand it to him at the voodoo ceremony."

"And you didn't tell me this before—why?"

"Because at the time I wasn't sure what I had seen. And it would be Holly's word against mine. But the pictures confirm her motivation for me."

"We want to get her to confess," Calista said.

"How?"

"I think I can do it," Eugenia added.

Rafe shook his head. "Not you."

"Yes, me. What? You think she's going to confess to Calista? Why would she? But I think she'll open up with me. I can go to see her wearing a . . . a wire, do you call it? You can be outside listening."

Rafe could see Cumberland considering the idea.

"All right," he clipped out.

Rafe was torn between victory and despair. He'd come over here thinking they could use Calista as the bait, but he knew that Eugenia was right. She was a better choice for the dangerous job because she was from the same social class as Holly. And she hadn't been fooling around with her husband, either.

"When were you planning to do this?" Cumberland asked.

"Tomorrow afternoon," Eugenia answered. She turned to Cumberland. "Can you be ready by then?"

"Yes." He looked at each of them. "And I don't want any strategy planning among the three of you tonight." He focused on Rafe. "I want you at your B&B. And I want Ms. Lacoste and Ms. Beaumont in their own beds. I will reinforce those restrictions with cops inside each of the women's homes to make sure you're not telephoning or e-mailing. Is that clear?"

"Yes," they all answered.

"We'll pick you up and drive you to the station house in the morning."

Rafe ached to have a few minutes alone with Eugenia, but Cumberland had made that impossible. He took one last look at her before a uniformed officer ushered him out of Calista's house. He'd thought he was being so clever when he'd suggested showing the pictures to the voodoo priestess. Now he'd put Eugenia in terrible danger, and he had no way of stopping the plot that he'd set in motion.

He let his police escort take him back to his room, when he wanted to spend the night with Eugenia, coaching her on how to handle Holly in this crucial confrontation. He prayed that he'd get a chance in the morning to give her some tips on how to deal with a woman who had already coolly murdered her husband in front of a bunch of witnesses and then convinced everyone that she was grieving.

Hating being out of the loop and knowing he had to find a way to relax, he put on his robe and practiced some strenuous martial arts moves until his muscles were screaming.

Finally he lay down, but his mind was still turning over

everything that had happened. Like Cumberland showing up at Calista's. Maybe after he knew Rafe had found the GPS on his car, he'd gone to more conventional methods—like a tag-team tail.

Of course there was no way to prove he'd been the one to put the tracking device on the car, and asking about it couldn't be a good idea.

Rafe set that aside, and finally he was able to sleep for a few hours.

When he arrived at the station house in the morning, he found Cumberland had already wired Eugenia for sound and given her some instructions for dealing with Holly. Then she got out her cell phone and dialed the widow.

He waited with his heart pounding as he listened to the phone ring. Finally Holly picked up, with the volume set so they could all hear.

"Eugenia?"

"Yes."

"What can I do for you?"

"You know that antiquing expedition we went on a couple of days ago?"

"Yes."

Rafe could tell she was struggling not to sound like she was on edge.

"There was a piece I saw that I was interested in. I went back and gave it a more careful look and found something in one of the drawers . . ." She stopped and started again. "I want to talk to you about it."

"Oh? What is it exactly?"

"I'd rather not talk about it over the phone. Can I come over?"

Holly hesitated for a moment. "Yes, if you think it's important."

"Would ten o'clock be too early?"

"No. That's fine."

Eugenia hung up and looked at her watch. "I've got to be there in a half hour."

Rafe had had all he could take. Without looking at any of the other people in the room, he put his arms around her and held her tightly. He felt her melt against him and dropped her head to his shoulder.

He stroked his hand down her back. "You're going to do great."

"I hope so."

"Just don't eat or drink anything while you're in there."

Eugenia's laugh was brittle.

He wanted to say, "I love you. For God's sakes be careful."

The first part jolted him. He had never admitted that before. Now he knew with absolute conviction that it was true.

Cumberland stepped forward. "Come on lovebirds. We have to get the show on the road."

Eugenia swallowed. "Yes."

The detective pressed a speed-dial button on his smartphone, and someone answered.

"Are you getting all that?"

"Loud and clear."

Eugenia flushed when she realized that she and Rafe

hadn't been talking only to the people in the room—they were also broadcasting to the technician who had wired her for sound.

They all trooped out to a white van with lettering proclaiming that it belonged to a rug-cleaning service. The interior was carpeted and there was a bench seat along one side. On the other side was a long desk filled with monitoring equipment, where a technician sat.

Eugenia sat up front with Cumberland. Rafe and Calista took the bench seat in back.

They drove toward Holly's house and stopped around the corner.

Cumberland got out and looked around, then opened the back door and motioned Eugenia out. "Show time."

"I want you to walk toward the house speaking in a low voice, and we'll keep doing sound checks. If we can't hear you, we'll use your phone vibrator."

Eugenia nodded.

Rafe forced himself to stay where he was as she picked up the folder with the pictures. And when she disappeared from sight, he felt his chest tighten. But he could still hear her reciting a recipe for shrimp etouffee. When she stopped speaking, his heart gave a hard thump. Then he heard a doorbell ring.

"Thanks for seeing me," Eugenia said.

"Come in."

This was another test of the sound system. The door closed behind Eugenia, and Holly said, "What's this about exactly?"

"It's kind of embarrassing,"

"Perhaps we should get comfortable."

They heard footsteps, and Rafe tried to imagine exactly where they were going in the house.

The two women began talking again.

"Can I offer you some tea?" Holly asked.

"No. I'm fine."

"Then why don't you tell me what's bothering you?"

He heard sounds of them moving around. Then Eugenia said. "I found some pictures in an old dresser I had delivered yesterday. They must have gotten caught in the underside of a drawer"

"Pictures of what?"

Eugenia must have passed them over, because they heard Holly make a gasping sound.

"Did you know your husband was into . . . that kind of thing?"

"No!"

"Are you sure?"

"Do you think I'm lying about something so disgusting?" Holly snapped.

"I think it would be pretty upsetting to suddenly discover this kind of activity. These are pictures of your husband and Calista, the voodoo priestess."

"I know who she is."

"But there were other girls. It looked like he'd been at it for a long time. How could he do that right under your nose?"

"Sometimes he took them out to our house near Jean Lafitte Park," she snapped, then sucked in a sharp breath.

"So you did know."

"I knew that bastard was more interested in his little honeypots than in me."

"That must have been very disturbing."

Holly made a sobbing sound. "It was humiliating. I was willing to do anything he wanted, but I wasn't young or pretty enough for him."

"That's awful."

"Yes," Holly sobbed out.

"I would have wanted to get even with him. How did you feel about it?"

"I hated him. I wanted him to pay for what he did, but I had to make it look like someone else wanted to harm him."

Rafe leaned forward, wishing he could see what was going on, but they only had the sound.

"Did you study voodoo poisons?" Eugenia asked.

"What—have you been checking up on me?"

"No, of course not. I'm on your side. I'm here because I know how disgusted you must have felt."

"I studied voodoo rituals. I'd go out to the country house when I knew Martin was away. And I'd pay Fortuna to keep quiet about my being there. But the rituals didn't do squat. I knew it was going to take more than sticking pins in a doll—or even killing a goat. I found an old recipe that seemed promising. I put it on one of the hors d'oeuvres at your restaurant the other night."

"That was clever of you."

"Don't patronize me. I'm sure you're here to collect evidence. Like the other day when you took me out for a visit to the antique shops. I'll bet you did it so that detective could get in here and snoop around. And now what are you up to? Are you planning to go to the police?"

"No," Eugenia denied.

"I can't let you do that."

Eugenia gasped. "You can't shoot me. Everybody will know you did it."

"No, you came over to harass me for ruining the reputation of your restaurant. You attacked me, and I had to shoot you."

CHAPTER TWENTY

Everything inside Rafe went cold.

Before Holly finished speaking, he was already out of the truck, running. Cumberland and a uniformed patrol officer were right behind him."

He ran with the speed of desperation, but before he reached the front door of Holly's house, he heard a shot.

When he tried to turn the knob, the door was locked.

Looking around for something to use as a battering ram, he picked up a cement planter on the porch and bashed it against the front door.

The barrier flew open and all three men charged into the house, following the sounds of a scuffle.

In the parlor, Eugenia was on the floor, struggling with Holly. The gun went off again, and Holly grunted.

Rafe grabbed Eugenia and pulled her away. Cumberland grabbed Holly.

When the two women were separated, he saw a red stain spreading across Holly's side.

"She's been hit. Get an ambulance."

"Already on the way," Cumberland said as he knelt over the older woman. He pulled up her blouse and looked at the blood that stained her ribs. "It's not life threatening."

Rafe turned Eugenia in his arms, holding on to her.

"Thank God you're all right," he breathed.

"I am, aren't I?" she asked, sounding surprised.

"How did you keep her from shooting you?"

She hesitated for a moment. I think it was harder for her to shoot me than poison her husband I figured I didn't have anything to lose by going in low and tackling her."

For the first time, Cumberland gave them a respectful look.

"And I guess you thought you had nothing to lose by letting us try for a confession," Rafe said to him.

"Yeah." He cleared his throat. "All's well that ends well."

Rafe refrained from making any editorial comments, and Cumberland gave them a few minutes together before he hauled them downtown to make statements.

When they'd finished writing their accounts, Rafe and Eugenia met near the front door.

"He wanted to know what the voodoo charm had to do with any of this," she said.

"What did you tell him?"

"That I didn't know. What did you say?"

"That I thought it was from someone who was trying to jinx your business."

"As good an answer as any."

She turned away to the desk clerk. "Do we get a ride home?"

"Yes, ma'am."

By the time a patrol car dropped them back at the restaurant, she was looking exhausted.

"Let the new staff you hired handle the restaurant tonight," Rafe said. "After the morning you've had, you're entitled to a night off."

She considered the suggestion and finally nodded. Her kitchen staff was already working, and she took a few minutes to discuss the menu with her sous-chef. Rafe watched her, impressed with her professionalism but feeling his nerves buzzing. He walked into the courtyard and sat down, knowing they had to start communicating better, but he had no idea how it was going to come out.

He stood up as Eugenia came into the courtyard.

"I'm finished." She cleared her throat. "We have to talk."

"I was thinking the same thing."

"You think we can have a productive conversation?"

He swallowed. "Yes."

She kept her gaze on him. "I think I know what might have happened to us."

"What?"

"Like you said when we saw Holly put the poison on the food, I can't prove anything."

"Maybe you can."

They both whirled to see Calista step through the doorway from the street.

"I'm glad I caught you together," she said. She'd been upset the night before, then been forced to follow Cumberland's game plan. Now she looked like her old self.

"I wasn't prepared for the conversation when you came over to my house last night," she said.

"Yeah," Rafe answered. "Sorry to hit you with those photos like that, but we needed your help."

She gave him a narrow-eyed look. "You wanted to jolt me, and you wanted me to confront Holly."

He spread his hands. "That was my plan."

"Thanks for admitting it." She paused a beat. "When you were starting to investigate the murders, you asked me who suggested doing Voodoo Night at a restaurant."

Rafe nodded.

"I thought back over the crowd at that fundraiser where I asked for questions written on cards. I'm pretty sure now that Holly was there. It was probably her—getting the ball rolling."

"Yeah."

She tipped her head to the side, studying him. "You claimed that you took Eugenia back in time to the ceremony where Villars died."

"It's not a claim. I did it."

"If you have that talent, I believe I have something that can help you."

"What?"

"A charm." She reached in her purse and took out a drawstring bag made of kente cloth. "See what the two of you can do with this."

"What are we *supposed* to do?" Eugenia asked.

"Sit down. Get comfortable and see where it takes you."

She handed the bag to Eugenia, then turned and left.

Eugenia weighed the bag in her hand. "Let's go up."

"And what?"

"Take her advice. What do we have to lose?"

He gave her a penetrating look. "I'm game if you are."

They went up and sat together on the sofa. Rafe had no idea what was going to happen but he pulled open the drawstring and took Eugenia's hand.

Then he gently shook the contents out onto the coffee table. They both studied the charm. It looked quite different from the evil thing that had been on Eugenia's doorstep after the voodoo ceremony.

He eyed it without picking it up. Perhaps its original purpose had been as a pincushion. It was a rounded silken mound, about three inches across, and it did appear to have short pins sticking in it. But each of them was topped with shiny beads and other baubles, some of which were heart-shaped. It had a jaunty, inviting appearance, although that could simply be a ruse.

"Interesting," Eugenia said. "Should we do it?"

"Yeah."

She clasped his hand more tightly as he reached for the charm.

The moment his fingers closed around the silky fabric, Eugenia felt dizzy.

With a shocked gasp, she tried to pull away from Rafe, but he held her fast.

"No," Eugenia cried out. But it was like the thing had taken control of her body—through Rafe.

The room around her faded into the background. She knew she was still sitting beside Rafe on the couch, but she was somewhere else, too. At first she felt like she was in an endless dark place where she couldn't catch her breath. Then, suddenly, it was like when she'd been in the restaurant with Rafe. Only she wasn't downstairs. She was standing in front of her house, the Victorian mansion in the Garden District where she'd grown up.

She knew she wasn't really there. She couldn't be. But it felt amazingly real. The view seemed to be from the side-walk, outside the wrought-iron fence.

It was summer, and flowers were blooming in the beds inside the fence—more than her mother planted these days.

As she watched, Mom came out, and Eugenia stared at her. She was younger, with less gray in her hair and firmer skin. It took a moment for Eugenia to realize that this must be years ago.

Actually, she knew about how long it had been because her mom walked to the old mailbox, the one she'd replaced the year Eugenia had gone away to the culinary school.

In the vision, Eugenia felt as if she were standing only a few feet away.

"Mom," she called out.

Her mother stopped short and looked around. She'd heard something, but it seemed that she saw no one.

"Who's there?"

Rafe squeezed her hand, and she knew he was still with her. "Don't try to interact with her. Just watch."

Her mother shook her head as though to clear it. Then

she opened the mailbox and took out the post—magazines, ads and envelopes.

Most of them were bills. One was clearly different, and when her mother came to it, her hand clenched.

Eugenia moved closer to have a look and froze when she saw it was addressed to her, and the name on the return address was Rafe Gascon.

She could hear Rafe's muffled exclamation.

"I told you I wrote to you."

Her mother paused and looked up, a wily expression on her face. She balled up the envelope and stuffed it into her pocket.

From the house, Eugenia heard herself call out anxiously, "Is there anything for me."

"No, dear."

When the scene around Eugenia started to fade, she tried to hold on to it. She wanted to know what had happened when her mother had come back into the house.

But the vision snapped off. Suddenly she was back in her own living room, blinking as the scene changed. And Rafe was beside her on the sofa, looking as shaken as she felt.

She saw his hand open and the charm drop to the table. Rafe had picked up the thing, and it had transported them back in time.

"You saw my mother take your letter and crumple it?" she whispered.

"Yes."

"And you heard her lie to me?"

"Yeah."

"After we both thought the other one didn't write, I

started wondering if she might have done something like that, but there was no way to prove it." She clenched her fists. "I want a confession—like with Holly."

"You think you can get it?"

"Maybe not. She's tough, but I'm going over to talk to her."

"Now?"

"Yes."

"Then I'm going with you."

"It's between me and her."

"If you want it that way, I'll stay out of the conversation, but I'm not letting you go alone." The way he said it left no room for argument.

She stood up, and Rafe escorted her down the steps. In the alley they climbed into his car, and headed for the Garden District, neither of them talking. Tension coursed through her, and she was sure it was the same for him.

He pulled to a stop in the driveway of the house where she'd grown up. Now that she was here, she knew she couldn't just barge in looking wild-eyed. On the porch, she pushed the button that activated the intercom.

"Mom. Are you there?"

"Eugenia?"

"I need to come in and talk to you. Where are you?"

"In the breakfast room."

She let herself and Rafe in, and they headed for the back of the house to the glassed-in room where her mother loved to sit and look out at her beautifully-landscaped backyard.

In the dining room, she turned to Rafe and said, "Wait here."

Her mother sat in a comfortable wicker chair; the trees outside in the yard diffused the sunlight.

Mom's hair had faded, but she kept a blond rinse on it. It hung loosely around her shoulders, in a style that had been basically the same for as long as Eugenia could remember.

She was wearing a simple A-line skirt, sandals, and an expensive white golf shirt. Not that she actually played golf.

When Mom had called after Villars' death hit the news, it hadn't been a very satisfactory conversation. Eugenia knew this was going to be worse.

Her mother closed the copy of Vogue in her lap and studied her daughter with appraising eyes, apparently reading the distress on her face.

"That voodoo priestess got you into trouble. Did you come to me for help mending things with Bennett? Really, you'd do better cooking in his restaurant."

"That's ridiculous."

"You'd have an advantage as a family business."

Right away, they'd gotten off on the wrong track, but she couldn't stop herself from saying, "Mom, Bennett hates me for doing better than he has."

"Of course not."

"He tried to make people think it wasn't safe to walk outside my restaurant at night."

"I don't believe it. He's my brother's son."

Eugenia sighed. Her mother had never been logical when she'd made up her mind about something.

"He was responsible for the muggings."

"How do you know?"

"He signed a confession."

"Under duress, I'm sure."

"That was after Rafe Gascon caught him trying to burn the trash in back of my restaurant."

"Rafe. You didn't mention him before. How is he mixed up in this?"

"He works for the detective agency I hired to find out who was responsible for the muggings."

Her mother snorted. "Like he could do anything besides fix broken toilets."

Eugenia worked to contain her rage. "He got a video of Bennett trying to burn down my restaurant a few nights ago."

"Did you see it?"

"No."

Before she could say more, Mom was speaking again. "He's probably lying to you."

"No he's not. He caught Bennett pouring charcoal lighter fluid into my trash cans."

"Or the Gascon boy did it himself."

Eugenia's voice turned hard as she stared at her mother. "What are you saying—that you think he hauled Bennett to the alley in back of my restaurant?"

Her mother didn't answer.

"We've gotten sidetracked. I came here to talk about when Rafe joined the army. We promised to write to each other, but you took his letters out of the mailbox and hid them, didn't you?"

Her mother had turned pale, but she wasn't about to confess the way Bennett had. "That's not true."

"Yes it is. And you didn't mail the ones I wrote him, either."

Her mother swallowed hard. "You're just guessing."

"No. It's true."

"How do you know?"

"Voodoo."

"Don't be ridiculous."

"You may think Calista caused trouble for me, but Martin Villars' death wasn't her fault."

Her mother made a sniffing sound.

"The good news is that she was willing to use her powers for me. She gave me a charm that showed me what you'd done. That's how I know about it."

"Oh come on. Voodoo is a bunch of hooey."

"No it's not. It showed me how far you'd go to ruin my life."

"I was doing you a favor. You were making a big mistake getting tangled up with that Gascon boy."

"So you admit it?"

"Why shouldn't I? I'm not ashamed of anything I've done."

"You had no idea of how much you were hurting us. You had no idea how he would turn out. He's a hardworking detective—and very good at his job. In fact, he saved my life." Before her mother could say anything else, she turned and left the room.

Her heart lurched when she saw the look on Rafe's face, but she kept walking until they were both out the front door, which she closed behind her.

Once outside, she ran down the steps and climbed into his car, then turned to him with tears in her eyes.

"She did that to us. I suspected it could be true. But now

I can hardly wrap my head around it." She gave him a pleading look. "Oh Rafe. I'm so sorry."

"She did it—not you."

"But we wasted all this time."

"We don't have to waste anymore." He reached for her and hauled her against himself.

"Rafe, as soon as you walked into the restaurant, I knew my feelings for you had never changed. But . . ."

"I wouldn't let you talk about . . . us."

"Why?"

He dragged in a breath and let it out. "I was trying to keep from getting hurt again."

She lifted her face, finding his lips with hers, wordlessly telling him how she felt. It was a kiss of passion, of understanding, and of apology for all the hurt they'd given each other.

"I'm sorry I doubted you," Rafe whispered when they finally broke apart.

"She made sure you did. But never again."

He took in her words, took in the reality of her in his arms—in his life. And there was more.

"I love you," she murmured.

He kept his gaze on her. "You don't know how I longed to hear that. After I came back, I kept myself from even admitting that I loved you. But I knew it before you went off to Holly's, and I wanted to tell you. Only there were too many people around."

"Oh Rafe."

"I loved you when we were together eight years ago. And now I know I never stopped, even when I couldn't admit it to myself."

"I loved you, too. And I was so sad when you left—when I thought you'd turned away from me." She gulped. "I even got married. That was the biggest mistake of my life."

"I know about that."

"How?"

"Well, I dropped you at your divorce lawyer's."

"Right. I wasn't even thinking about that."

"It was in your file that Frank Decorah gave me."

"Are you angry?"

"How can I be angry? You were trying to live your life."

"But Richard was absolutely wrong for me. I knew it pretty soon after we married."

"And I'm selfishly glad you figured it out."

She pressed her mouth to his and spoke against his lips. "He could never compare to you. Not as a man and not as a lover. You were so much better at it—even with what we were doing."

"I always wanted you to enjoy what we were doing as much as I did."

She reached for his hand and squeezed it. "Am I going to be the one who asks where this is leading now?"

He swallowed hard, still half afraid that the dream would slip away. "To marriage, I hope."

"Oh yes."

She kissed him again, cutting off the conversation.

"How are we going to work it out?"

"I'm sure I can transfer to our New Orleans office." He laughed. "Maybe that's what Frank Decorah had planned. He's a devious old matchmaker, although he wouldn't admit it, if you asked him." He looked around realizing they were still in front of her mother's house. "Let's get out of here."

"Yes."

As he drove away, she leaned back, her hand on his arm, her eyes closed, and a smile on her face. When the car came to a stop, she looked around.

"Where are we?"

"My bed and breakfast. Neutral territory."

"Why?"

"Because I know that if we go back to the restaurant, you're going to want to stop in the kitchen and then check the dining room. And I want your full attention."

She nodded. "I guess you know me pretty well."

He parked in the lot out back, then led her inside to his first-floor room with its classic English furnishings and a view of a pretty interior garden.

"What a great room," she murmured.

"I thought you'd like it. I kept dreaming of bringing you back here."

He crossed to the window and closed the drapes, then drew her into his arms.

Her head dropped to his shoulder, and for long moments he absorbed the reality of holding her close, now that he knew everything was all right between them.

Her fingers tangled in his hair, stroked across his broad back, drifted to curve around his ass. Loving the possessive way she touched him, he bent to stroke his cheek against hers, then covered her mouth with his.

As his lips moved over hers, he was caught by a flood of emotions, all the hunger he'd tried to contain finally given free rein.

She raised her face and found his lips.

"Oh Rafe. It's really true. I have you back again. I can hardly believe it."

"It's true. Finally." He ended the words with a kiss that was full of passion and promise. She tasted wonderful, felt wonderful in his arms, and he gathered her close.

He wanted to say so much to her, but he was too overwhelmed to speak. Instead he led her to the bed, where they began to slowly, teasingly undress each other. Her blouse and skirt. His jeans and polo shirt. Her bra and panties. His shorts.

And when they were both naked, they swayed in each other's arms, touching and kissing and letting themselves enjoy the moment. When he knew he could no longer stand, he pulled back the brocade spread and took her down to the surface of the bed, gathering her to him, rocking with her as they continued to give and take pleasure in each other, wrapping themselves in incredible sensual pleasure.

He cupped her breasts, loving their warmth and fullness. Easing away, he took one hardened nipple in his mouth, sucking on her as he teased its mate with his thumb and finger. The attentions wrung a glad cry from her.

Making love with her had been a dream fulfilled. Commitment made it even better.

His free hand traveled downward to dip into her hidden folds, where he found her hot and slick and ready for him.

"Rafe, please," she moaned, "Please, I want you inside me. I need you inside me—now."

As she spoke, her hand closed around the hard, distended shaft of his cock, sending a jolt of pure, animal sensation surging through him.

He rolled to his back, lifting her up, setting her over him. Her gaze never left his as she plunged down, bringing him inside her.

He took in her beautiful body as she began to move above him, knowing that she had never been this open, this free with him before.

She went still, smiling down at him.

"Finally, finally, after all this long time, you belong to me," she whispered.

"And you to me."

"Oh Rafe," she breathed, as she began to move again. He matched her rhythm, wanting to draw out the incredible pleasure but knowing he was too far gone to last for long. He felt her inner muscles contract, heard her call out his name once more. And then he was shaking with the force of his own release, incredible pleasure washing over him.

Afterwards she came down beside him, and he held her in his arms, enjoying the satisfied expression on her face.

"Something I want to say."

He tensed. "Yes?"

"Before you joined the army, I was going to tell you I'd sleep with you, if you stayed."

He was stunned. "But you didn't."

"I decided that wasn't fair to you. You'd made a decision about your life, and I couldn't hold you here with sex."

He laughed. "Maybe you could have. But this is better. We both grew up. And I've got a profession. I'm not the lowlife kid with nothing to offer you."

"I never thought of you as a lowlife kid."

"But it wouldn't have worked. Not then."

"Maybe not," she said as she snuggled against him, then lifted her hips so he could free the covers and pull them up.

As he clasped her to him, he was happier than he had ever been in his life, yet he knew it was only the beginning of what the two of them would mean to each other.

ALSO BY REBECCA YORK

SCIENCE FICTION ROMANCE

Off-World Series

Hero's Welcome (an off-world series short story)

Nightfall (an off-world series novella)

Conquest (an off-world series short story)

Assignment Danger (an off-world novella)

Christmas Home (an off-world short story)

Firelight Confession (an off-world novella)

Escape Velocity

PARANORMAL ROMANTIC SUSPENSE

Decorah Security Series

On Edge (a Decorah Security prequel novella)

Dark Moon (a novel)

Dark Powers (a novel)

Rx Missing (a novel)

Found Missing (a novel)

Hunter (a novel)

Trapped (a novel)

Scene of the Crime (a novel)

Hollow Moon (a novella)

Fire on the Moon (a novel)

Terror Mansion (a novella)

ABOUT THE AUTHOR

A New York Times and USA Today Best-Selling Author, Rebecca York is a 2011 recipient of the Romance Writers of America Centennial Award. Her career has focused on romantic suspense, often with paranormal elements.

Her 16 Berkley books and novellas include her nine-book werewolf "Moon" series. KILLING MOON was a launch book for the Berkley Sensation imprint. She has written over 50 books for Harlequin Intrigue, many in her popular 43 Light Street series.

She has written for Harlequin, Berkley, Dell, Tor, Carina Press, Silhouette, Kensington, Running Press, Tudor, Pageant Books, Scholastic, and Sourcebooks.

Her many awards include two Rita finalist books. She has two Career Achievement awards from Romantic Times: for Series Romantic Suspense and for Series Romantic Mystery. And her Peregrine Connection series won a Lifetime Achievement Award for Romantic Suspense Series.

Many of her novels have been nominated for or won RT

Reviewers Choice awards. In addition, she has won a Prism Award, several New Jersey Romance Writers Golden Leaf awards and numerous other chapter awards.

Oliver Heber Books is now publishing her Decorah Security Series, her Off World Series, and her Soulmated Series.

www.ingramcontent.com/pod-product-compliance
Lightning Source LLC
Chambersburg PA
CBHW05030711072 6
47899CB00007B/2141